THE
EXILE
OF
CÉLINE

TOM CLARK

THE EXILE OF CÉLINE

RANDOM HOUSE
NEW YORK

Library of Congress Cataloging-in-Publication Data

Clark, Tom, 1941–
The exile of Céline.

1. Céline, Louis-Ferdinand, 1894–1961, in fiction,
drama, poetry, etc.   2. World War, 1939–1945—Fiction.
I. Title.
PS3553.L29E9   1987   843'.912   86-10234
ISBN 0-394-55312-8

MANUFACTURED IN THE UNITED STATES OF AMERICA
2 3 4 5 6 7 8 9
FIRST EDITION

TYPOGRAPHY AND BINDING DESIGN BY BARBARA M. BACHMAN

to Angelica

We should, so we are told, eschew evil
and, if possible, neither touch nor mention
it. For evil is also the thing of ill omen,
that which is tabooed and feared. This attitude towards evil, and the apparent cir-
cumventing of it, flatter the primitive ten-
dency in us to shut our eyes to evil and
drive it over some frontier or other, like
the Old Testament scapegoat, which was
supposed to carry the evil into the wilderness.

—C. G. JUNG

Me thought I heard a voyce cry,
Sleep no more.

—*Macbeth* (II.2)

THE EXILE OF CÉLINE

1.

SAUVE QUI PEUT

n a gray wintry day in November 1944, a welcoming party of French fascist collaborators stood on the railway platform at Sigmaringen, an ancient Hohenzollern town on the Danube that had become the last haven of the fallen Vichy government.

Stomping well-worn boot heels to keep warm, they exchanged anticipatory glances. Due to arrive on the incoming train was Dr. Ferdinand Destouches, better known as Louis-Ferdinand Céline—physician, author of famous novels and once (in a series of inflammatory pamphlets) France's most outspoken herald of Aryan supremacy. Céline and his wife Lucette were now fleeing for their lives—headed toward Denmark, where the doctor-writer had stashed his assets in gold. This erratic odyssey, a voyage full of hardships, setbacks and delays, had so far taken almost half a year, and was still far from over.

A whistle sounded, not far off. Over the tinny loudspeaker, the arrival of the Ulm local was announced in German, then in French.

The train was not much to speak of: an old, laboring locomotive, some flatcars carrying military hardware, a single passenger carriage. The collaborators pressed forward, eager to greet the one man who—so it was said—still had the strength of spirit to represent France with pride in its hour of ignominy.

As Céline stepped down apprehensively, looking both ways, the circuitous route he had taken through Germany showed its effects on his face. Those deep Breton-blue eyes, whose depths had always spoken of oceans of sorrow and distress, were now flat and staring, almost feral in their apparent detachment from the human. His slightly unbalanced features, the left eye half closed, the left side of the mouth drawn up, usually created an involuntary satirical expression; now the impression was exaggerated by extreme exhaustion. His graying hair was long and wild. Three days' growth of beard dusted his sunken cheeks, whose pallor gave the skin a texture like old ivory. He wore a cloth engineer's cap, several ragged and badly faded aviator's jackets piled one over the other and a pair of huge, greasy, moth-eaten dark blue trousers. On his thin legs, these baggy trousers created a clownish effect that was enhanced by enormous hand muffs, lined with animal skin, which dangled from a frayed string around his neck. The layers of nondescript apparel gave his half-starved frame the bulk of an ocean diver's. In a sack slung over his stomach there were two or three airholes, obviously cut by hand, through which you could see parts of what was evidently a very large and completely motionless tabby cat.

The sight of Céline in this seedy condition was an obvious disappointment to the collaborators. They exchanged deflated glances.

One of them, the writer Lucien Rebatet, stepped forward. "Your baggage?"

Céline nodded toward Lucette, who was climbing down from the carriage. Loaded with sacks and slings like a coolie, she nonetheless appeared trim and well groomed, as if the months of makeshift living hadn't fazed her. Her high, broad forehead, emphasized by the way she'd swept her long hair back away from it, and her large, watchful eyes suggested the observant expression of an intelligent forest creature.

Rebatet helped the travelers get their baggage into a French militia staff car, and rode along as Céline and Lucette were driven through the narrow streets of the quaint old town of Sigmaringen. When the car passed under the enormous Hohenzollern castle, Rebatet pointed out a remote turret, over a hundred feet in the air.

"Up there at the top—seventh story—Pétain's got a suite. He rarely comes out. He's got his own doctor, so you probably won't see him. After that little joke in your pamphlet about his being a Jew, it's probably just as well! The generals and admirals are up there with him. And on the floors below, the ministers, Bonnard, Gabolde, Déat, Brinon, Bridoux, Darnand, Marion . . ."

"Lucifer and his fallen angels," Céline interjected, "in a gingerbread hell! And Laval?"

"He's up there next to Pétain. They're kept apart by a stone wall, of course. Pétain won't talk to him—or to anyone. That's the way things are here: every man for himself!"

Lucette looked out at the pink-and-pistachio-colored houses. "It's pretty, at least."

"A town made out of stucco pastry," Céline put in acidly, "with that castle for a wedding cake on top. The perfect setting for lyric opera."

"If you knew what went on in there . . ." Rebatet began. "It's more like a play by one of the lesser Elizabethans: vengeance, foul plots, assassinations and treachery among friends. And it's coming down to the last act."

"The last act," Céline said, "has already been written. Hitler will drag us all through the pearly gates with him. We haven't any choice, do we, Rebatet?"

"But you've always kept your distance."

"There's no distance left! His war has become our war. And look how he's fought it. With ideas straight out of the 1870s. The old imperial battle plan! Total war! As obsolete as military bands and oil paintings of battleships. But not to Herr Hitler. His idea of technique is to be absolutely predictable. Build up a big army at one weak spot, break through, surround them with armor! Mechanical and crude, wouldn't you say? The work of a quantitative mind . . . Hitler's a positivist, you see. No imagination, no capacity for surprise! He stumbled into a total war that's turned out to be a war of industry, which he can't win because he's outnumbered. It's obvious he knows nothing about his opponents. That's because he's provincial. He knows less about the British and the Russians than any schoolboy would. He underestimated the stubbornness of the British upper classes. He let them off just when he had Churchill by the balls. Then he provoked the Americans, a terrible and unnecessary mistake. And worst of all, he underestimated the Red Army. Somebody should have told him you can't fight Russia without *belief.* Mere technique's not enough!"

"The generals are very displeased with him, it's said."

"Hitler's never been anything but a drummer. His function is simply to beat the drum while the stupidity of the German bourgeoisie marches us all into the arms of Stalin."

"Merde!" The militiaman at the wheel swerved to keep from hitting a mangy-looking dog that was lapping up some dirty water spilled on the cobblestone street.

They pulled up in front of the Löwen, a small hotel so antiquated it had developed a slight tilt. The castle towered over it, keeping the lopsided little hotel in permanent shadow.

A German military car waited outside. Just as Rebatet, Céline and Lucette were entering, two huge, menacing German shepherds surged out of the hotel, tugging along a soldier who was barely able to restrain them with a leash. Behind him a heavyset man in the long leather coat of a German officer came out. The officer nodded curtly to Rebatet.

"This is our new doctor," Rebatet said to him. And to Céline, "This is Gauleiter Boemelburg, S.S. Sturmbahnführer of Sigmaringen."

"Ah?" Boemelburg regarded the new arrival with sudden curiosity. "You're Céline the writer?"

"Yes."

"We'll be neighbors, I hear."

The dogs began barking and snarling. Céline stepped back.

Half an hour later Céline and Lucette sat dismally in the midst of their half-unpacked baggage. They'd hardly expected first-class accommodations, but the tiny, dingy hotel room was a disappointment nonetheless. Lucette glanced around in dismay at the cracked plaster, the mildewed wallpaper, the broken windows. Gray loops of stuffing leaked out of the arm of her chair like the intestines of a gutted sheep.

Bébert, released from his rucksack, was sniffing around in the room's dark corners. Suddenly his paw shot out. He'd trapped a cockroach. He pounced on it, then seemed to lose interest. The insect escaped, scurrying under the bed.

"You see how magnanimous Bébert is, Luci? He knows that cockroach has got a family to feed!"

Back propped against the head of the bed, Céline was using a small penknife to undo the stitching that secured the lining of one of his jackets. Reaching inside, he withdrew a brown-paper packet, opened it and dropped the contents on the bedcover. There were two passports, some gold coins, a syringe and several small vials, each containing either morphine or cyanide.

Lucette shivered. She got up, walked to one of the windows. It had an old-fashioned casement frame. Three small panes were missing. She toyed with the splintered woodwork of the frame. "We must cover this with paper. The wind comes in!"

"Yes." He was now busy cleaning the syringe with alcohol.

She turned to him. "And what are we supposed to eat in this place?"

He daubed the needle with a cotton swab. "We're to be given some food cards."

"For dinners of potato soup, like in Kränzlin?"

"Where there's a war, there's a black market. That's one thing we can count on, Luci."

She didn't reply. Instead, she began doing pliés. Dipping quickly at the knees, she looked as graceful as ever, belying the years that had passed since her last performance as a professional dancer.

Céline sat watching her exercise, his mind floating back over visions of other women he'd observed at their physical training. Lucette was only the latest of his dancer-lovers. Many had come before. A woman's voice drifted into his head. *"Ein, zwei, drei."* It belonged to a Viennese gymnastics teacher he had known—an agreeable woman, and sensitive as well . . . hadn't she been a friend of Freud's? He hadn't heard from her for several years now. She was Jewish; he wondered what had happened to her.

The doctor ministered to the medical needs of nearly two thousand French exiles. For the first few weeks he was forced to practice in his own room at the Löwen. His patients, many of them afflicted with unpleasant contagious diseases, had to be examined on the same bed Céline and Lucette slept in; there was simply nowhere else to put them. Later he was given the use of a consulting room vacated by a local physician who'd been called up for military duty. The tiny office was in a building on the bank of the Danube, under the shadow of the castle. It was filthy, and drastically under-equipped; any medical tools and supplies left behind by the German doctor had long since been plundered.

Not even at his night clinic in France, inundated with tubercular industrial workers, had Céline practiced in conditions like this. He saw sick people all day in this impromptu "office," and made private calls at all hours of the night. His patients ranged from ministers and generals, whose symptoms he attributed mostly to old sins of excessive eating and drinking, to lower-level collaborators, military men, civil servants and members of the militia—among whom a clinically rich spectrum of venereal infections spoke of more recent vices.

The endless stream of cases of crabs and clap through his consulting room afforded the doctor a close study of human ethics in time of stress. The upshot was another ironic entry in his mental notebook on the decline of the species. "A joke, really," he remarked to Lucette, "the amount of last-ditch togetherness exhibited by this race whose individuals demonstrate their most intense mutual attraction just before extermination!"

He was liable to be summoned at any hour to the castle, the hotels or the Fidelis, a local convent converted into a hospital by the Germans. It was a hospital straight out of Hieronymus Bosch. A visit to the Fidelis, with its perpetual circus of pregnant women and sick children, was an ordeal that always lasted hours: The place was one big dormitory of pallets, with colics and fevers everywhere. Even so, Céline battled with the authorities to keep his patients there rather than have them transferred to the nearby German-run "maternity camp" at Siessen, where conditions were even worse; infant mortality rates at Siessen were about what they would have been in the wilds of nature.

The general health of the French community at Sigmaringen seemed to decline along with its morale. There were ailing cabinet ministers all over town to care for, and the overloaded passenger trains that arrived every day at the station were often carrying young women in labor or older ones with legs so badly swollen from the voyage they were unable to walk. Faced with a work load that would have been a heavy burden for any hospital staff, the doctor rarely rested and was never paid; his patients, many of whom suspected him of disloyalty to the fascist cause, were just as likely to spit in his face. When he walked through the narrow streets of the old town on medical calls—armed with a hunter's game bag as his doctor's kit, his pockets crammed with prescriptions held together by a large safety pin—the local children, starved-looking bands of ragamuffins, often pelted him with stones.

Understandably preoccupied with losing a war, the German military management left the French population to heal itself. It was, one Nazi officer told Céline, a matter of survival of the fittest.

There were urgent shortages of essential medicines—sulfur creams, camphorated oil, gardenal, digitalin, morphine, ether. Céline procured these by dipping into his escape funds, slipping handfuls of francs to the pharmacist at the *hofapothek*. On the black market he bought German morphine and thermometers shipped from Switzerland.

The doctor applied for help and supplies from the French colony at Constance, where Jacques Doriot dominated a second collaborationist enclave. Doriot was raising his own army to re-take France—with a little help from Hitler. He had rivals at Sigmaringen. Supplying Céline with medicines was not a high priority for Doriot. Céline, however, did manage to recruit a medical orderly from Constance, one of Doriot's own men—an eccentric patriot and veteran of the Russian front named Germinal Chamoin. A former cook at the McAlpin Hotel in New York (where Céline had once stayed while on tour), Chamoin had narrowly escaped death at Stalingrad: when he could no longer stand up in the snow, he'd been sent back home.

Chamoin proved invaluable. He provided the doctor not only with the services of an aide, but with a spiritual foil and ally, a companion of the abyss. To Céline, Chamoin's experiences in the East qualified him as an authentic seer. Stalingrad, the doctor believed, was not just the end of the war, it was the end of Europe.

"They shipped you out of the deep freeze just in time," he told Chamoin one day as they were doling out salves to militiamen in his office. "Just before it turned into an icicle in Hitler's aorta."

"There were many of us who wished Hitler had been there," the orderly said. "He'd have found out what it feels like to have a heart."

Céline let out a short, bitter laugh. "It doesn't take a heart to read the writing on the wall. From Stalingrad on, the whole thing was . . ." He made a quick cutting gesture at his own throat. "Oh yes, it's over and done with, this civilization of whites. It doesn't matter what the collabos think. Condemned men will believe in any chimera, eh? No, Chamoin, you and I know better. All that's left is the noise. The bubbles of fire, the rockets, the cataracts!"

The militiamen who stood in line to be treated for scabies exchanged anxious glances. Everybody said the doctor was a head case, but how could you tell for sure?

"Next," said Céline. "Down with the trousers!"

Stranded in the tiny hotel room while Céline made his endless rounds, Lucette grew more and more restless. She had no place to dance, so Céline lobbied for space with one or two of the ministers whom he saw on medical visits. Before long, Lucette was given permission to take daily exercise in the Portuguese Gallery, a large ballroom at the castle. The ballroom had neither heat nor ventilation. Lucette would fling open the French doors that led out to a balcony. Wind and sometimes snow blew through the room.

There was a large rococo mirror in front of which she could work. In tights and ballet slippers, she danced to the music of a small, tinny phonograph.

One day a general in full uniform exploded into the ballroom. He strode across the parquet floor with a loud clatter of jackboots, bearing down on the startled Lucette. It was the Vichy minister of war, General Bridoux, trailed by an aide-de-camp.

Snow flurries were drifting into the ballroom.

"What's going on here?" General Bridoux demanded. "Who opened those doors?"

Lucette looked up at him sheepishly but said nothing.

The general scanned her with distaste. "If you like fresh air so much, dance outside." He turned to the aide. "Do something about this!"

The aide scurried off and began shutting all the doors.

Lucette went outside onto the balcony. There, overlooking the town and the pine forest beyond (where small, Bruegelesque groups of figures, the French work parties assigned to wood foraging by the Nazis, could be seen dragging tree trunks through the snow) she continued her arabesques and pirouettes.

For its temporary French residents, Sigmaringen was a Russian-roulette game of discretion, indirection, endless double and triple entendres. Scheming with or against your fellow inmate—for Sigmaringen was also a prison in the sense that you couldn't leave—had become so ingrained by the time of Céline's arrival that his refusal to participate in it made him seem an absolute anomaly, somehow both more and less than human in a time when to be a man meant to be an illustration out of a book by Machiavelli or Thomas Hobbes.

One cold clear night a little party of Vichy ministers, collaborationist intellectuals, and their wives, out strolling in the castle gardens, stopped to investigate some soft noises that seemed to emanate from a bush. It sounded to them at first like lightly running water, then when they got closer they could make out a male voice. In the middle of the bushes a man down on his knees extended one arm, with fingers splayed, toward a cat—which extended one of its own forepaws, claws sheathed, toward him. The man crooned softly, the cat purred back, their voices joined in a single low, vibrant tone. A tender epiphany under the moonlight, and a strange one. The ministers, collaborators and their wives quietly withdrew. The man down on his knees was the peculiar medical man, Dr. Destouches, who, it was sometimes said, got along far better with animals than he did with human beings.

The black market was the supermarket of Sigmaringen. Buying and selling was the principal sport of the town, but it required a ready supply of goods. Switzerland was the source. Butter, thermometers, Gitanes, "Rhine wines," salami: You couldn't get them in German shops, but for the right price, you could pay somebody to bring them in over the snows. By this route Céline obtained not only medical supplies and drugs for his patients, but foodstuffs to supplement the meager rations he and Lucette were allocated by the Nazis. So active was his participation in the black market, in fact, that he felt constrained to take pains to conceal it from even the literary collaborators, like Lucien Rebatet. "One word in the wrong place," he told Lucette, "and it's the end for us." Now and then they made a show of joining Rebatet and the others at hotels where the Germans provided a nightly fare of thin broth. Céline and Lucette forced themselves to swallow the rutabaga-and-red-cabbage soup, but their performance was undercut by the obviously well-fed Bébert. After one disdainful sniff at the foul-smelling stuff, he ostentatiously turned up his nose.

The buccaneers of the black market plied their trade in a dead zone between nations. They were bizarre characters with false names and shifting nationalities. Belgians, Hungarians, Luxemburgers, Arabs, Jews, they came into Sigmaringen with cigarettes, flashlights, English tea, sulfur medicines. You placed your orders in advance, in cash. Of course, sometimes you handed over your money, then never saw the supplier again. It was one of the hazards of the sport.

One morning in December, Céline was summoned to the castle to see Brinon, one of the principal ministers. He ran into the usual crowd of hungry refugees milling around the main gate, a vast portal wide enough for sixteen imperial horsemen to pass through. On his first visit to the castle, Céline had dubbed it "The Gate of *The Sign of Zorro*," because it was the kind of castle entrance you'd see in a Hollywood movie. "And you expect to see the blond head of a damsel up there in the turrets," he'd told Lucette.

Inside, he made his way through the labyrinth of lower corridors to the upper halls, where the twenty-five Vichy ministers had suites of rooms. Along the walls, among the trophies and banners and ornamental hangings, were paintings of the former Hohenzollern landlords, masters of the castle down through the centuries. The doctor paused to commune briefly with one of them, a hammer-faced prince of the early sixteenth century. "An ugly mug like that," he said to himself, "always goes with money." He hurried along, up the corkscrew stairways, past the armor-plated statues: no reason to make a minister impatient, you could lose your food card that way.

"Graf von Brinon": the placard on Brinon's door, in Gothic lettering. Céline sneered and knocked lightly.

Fernand de Brinon, a former journalist, was now an important man in the castle, hand in hand with his Nazi hosts. He was president, in fact, of the Commission for the Interests of French Subjects in Germany, a position of some power, although the commission itself was not formally recognized by Laval, the erstwhile president of France; nor by Marshal Pétain, who kept himself in a seven-room suite, aloof from Nazis and other ministers alike; nor by the black marketeers, who gave no discounts to politicians. Brinon had six food cards, it was said, or perhaps seven; eight at the most. (Pétain, at the top of the pecking order of exiles, commanded eighteen.) That gave him more butter than a cellful of civil servants, but not enough wine and cigarettes to suit his taste.

Céline found him in a dressing gown, smoking, looking distraught. Brinon was not an outgoing man. "Animal of the shadows," Céline called him. He was quiet, secretive and regarded as extremely dangerous. Pétain, Laval and the other ministers—most of whom cultivated an attitude of remoteness toward the Germans—gave him a wide berth. A wrong word from Brinon could put you on a one-way trip to the Black Forest in a taxi with darkened windows.

Madame Mitre, Brinon's sinuous and elegant mistress, offered Céline a seat; he dutifully settled into a seventeenth-century brocade chair but turned down her offer of a cigarette.

"You know, doctor," said Brinon, attempting light conversation before getting to his point, "it was I who had the honor of doing the first French interview with the Führer."

"I should think you'd be trying to suppress that fact."

"My dear fellow, it would be one of the proud moments of anyone's life, meeting a man like that."

Céline sniffed. "I'd just as soon he'd died in Flanders. I know better men who did. For that matter, I'd have been lucky to die there myself, as things turned out. But I was only wounded instead. The whole experience left me disgusted. Hitler got promoted, so it left him inspired."

"But I've read your pamphlets; he seems to have inspired *you*."

"That was simply vanity. I said the Boches were our only defense against the Russians. He was saying the same thing. I should have kept my mouth shut."

"Come now, doctor, you must consider yourself fortunate to be here!"

"Fortunate?" Céline emitted a dry laugh. "Hardly."

"Have you considered what might have happened to you if you'd stayed in Paris?" The thought didn't seem to trouble Brinon, who stared absently up into the beams and wainscoting of the ceiling.

Céline's eyes glinted. "Oh, that was no secret. They made it plain to me—the heroes of the Resistance. Nothing but thugs and vandals! They smashed my motorcycle, they sent me little coffins in the mail. I suppose you've never received one of those? And the BBC! 'Monster of Montmartre, we will cut you up into little pieces. . . .' Not very reassuring, I can tell you."

"So you see how much better off you are here." Brinon waved a soft white hand around the room, taking in the casement windows through which the Danube sparkled icy-blue and poster-pretty against the pines beyond.

"Oh, nothing's changed! In Paris they wanted to tear my eyes out, kill me. Here it's the same. A different set of thugs, that's all."

"You're imagining things!"

"I only observe what's *real*. It's necessary for me to see what's going on around me because I've put myself in jeopardy from all directions at once. I've been an idiot; I've mixed myself up in history, all because I was vain—I thought I was saving France."

Brinon smiled. "As we all did. That's why we're here."

"No, I just picked the wrong side. Marion said to me yesterday: 'If you'd stuck with the Left, they'd have a whole floor of suites booked for you at the Excelsior.' Instead I'm up to my neck in shit."

"I understand your sentiments." Brinon's tone was cool.

"Oh, it's a good thing you can't read my thoughts."

"But you do very little to conceal them, doctor."

"You can't have brought me here to tell me that."

"Of course not, it's about these children at the Fidelis— they're being sent to Siessen."

The doctor sprang from his chair, which squeaked against the rosewood parquet floor, but before he could say a word Brinon remarked blandly: "The care in German hospitals is quite good."

"Starving children on runny carrot soup is not my idea of generosity." Céline felt his voice shaking, despite himself. "You know, I've seen some sanitary abuses in my time—on three continents! In Africa, and then among the brutalized workers *chez* Ford . . . Not to mention the Stone Age obstetrics and gynecology department of the Supreme Soviet Hospital for Venereal Diseases in Leningrad, where I saw cervical examinations performed bare-handed by doctors who told me there wouldn't be any rubber gloves until the completion of the latest Five-Year Plan. But I've never seen anything as inhuman, or as vicious, as the medical hygiene of these so-called allies of ours."

Brinon glared. "Calm down. The Germans are our only hope, as Frenchmen."

Céline forced himself back into his chair and stared past Brinon's well-groomed head at the embroidered draperies, which displayed images of stags, serfs, horses and red-hatted riders carrying hunting horns. The riders wore tunics designed with bees, eagles and the Hohenzollern coat of arms. A world where cruelty is routine has no need for hygiene, Céline commented silently to himself. His habitual obsequious smile was twisted by contempt, but he didn't speak.

"I'm sure the children will get better care in Siessen than they are receiving here," said Brinon.

"I'm doing what I can for them, without any help from our hosts," Céline said. "As for what happens at Siessen, you know as well as I do, it's mere infanticide, Grand Guignol, phony medical sideshows—an organized morgue, in fact. Really," he gestured at the decor, "it smacks of these Hohenzollerns, the kind of tricks they pulled in the old days."

"I'm sorry, doctor, it can't be helped. You'll have to sign the certificate." Brinon paused, glancing toward his watchful consort, Madame Mitre. "And another matter. These government people of ours, they're becoming a serious nuisance with their constant scratching. It's not civilized."

"And even at dinner," put in Madame Mitre. She took a cigarette from a gold case, lit it and exhaled smoke in the doctor's direction.

"It's the crabs," Céline shrugged, making a face.

"Can't you do something about it?" Brinon asked curtly.

"Not without the ointments from Switzerland."

"You know the commission has no medical allocation for the black market."

Céline eyed the swastika over Brinon's dresser. "Perhaps you ought to ask your Führer. Tell him you need sulfur to keep the hands of the allies of Germany out of their pockets at dinner. Who knows, perhaps he'll send you a million francs."

"Well then, we can't afford it," sighed Brinon, shaking his head. "Let them scratch."

"As in a zoo!" Madame Mitre's upper lip curled back in distaste, exposing fine teeth through which smoke issued in thin wisps that reminded Céline of dry ice.

"Don't worry," he said. "There are ways . . . I suppose I could get a kilo of the ointment from one of the *passeurs*. I've got certain connections, as you know."

Brinon's relief was apparent. "It's only one of the reasons we value your presence here, doctor. It makes it possible for us to overlook some of these medical reports of yours." Brinon glanced at him sidelong. "And speaking of your connections, there's another matter I'd like to discuss with you, doctor. These friends of yours, do you think they could get their hands on a decent shortwave radio for me?"

"I suppose, for the right price."
"And cognac, two bottles . . . and Lucky Strikes?"

The waning of the year brought a brief flurry of hope: von Rundstedt's Ardennes offensive. The desperate collaborators at Sigmaringen, now clutching at every straw, searched for signs in the smallest scrap of news from the front. Coming away from informal conferences with their German hosts, they clacked hopefully among themselves, like geese in a game bag who convince themselves they're smelling the familiar farmyard even as they're slung toward the chopping block.

A meeting of French collaborationist intellectuals—Abel Bonnard, Vichy minister of education, Lucien Rebatet and others—took place in the town hall in December. It had been arranged by a Nazi official who admired Céline's books; the same official had also been instrumental in bringing him to Sigmaringen. The gathering was intended to cement Franco-Nazi relations, with Céline as feted guest.

German generals and functionaries turned out for the occasion. Cooks from the castle had provided a dinner that was less meager than usual. There was an unexpected fish entrée. Lined up on a mahogany table, silver trays of bright pink salmon were surrounded by bottles of red wine, arranged like destroyers around a battleship. The wine was plentiful, and most of the French guests were in their cups before dinner was over.

As his fellow countrymen, making the compulsory speeches, fell all over one another in their zeal to please the German hosts, Céline looked on with undisguised contempt. Finally he took to his feet and began to speak. At first he employed the mocking, bantering tone familiar to those who'd known him in Paris. Soon, though, there was a new edge in it, which got sharper as he continued to talk. The Germans, who understood less clearly Céline's unusual mix of street slang and burlesque imagery, continued to chuckle even when the Frenchmen in the audience had grown rigid and silent.

At the climax of his speech, Céline diagnosed the collaborators' condition with icy succinctness: "You're nothing but fuckups, you've thrown away your honor, they've taken away your property, now you're about to lose your lives, and all you can think about is pouring alcohol down your gullets! At least the Germans can hold their heads up. They may go home beaten, but they've done their patriotic duty. Whereas all you've done is gorge yourselves. Everything on the house! It's a ceremony of cunts—on the way to the cemetery! I propose that we forget about forming a society of Franco-German intellectuals and instead form a society of the Friends of Père Lachaise!"

Medals clattered on the chests of guffawing German generals. Of course Céline's speech was part of the scheduled entertainment, wasn't it? The generals weren't noticing the frosty silence that had fallen over the French contingent.

Céline went on, saliva trickling from the corners of his mouth as always happened when he got excited. "And what's worse, how could there be any excuse for you, as Frenchmen, not only getting involved in this fucked-out disaster of a war, but collaborating with a bunch of mugs who wear the uniform of your ancient enemy—the uniform you ought to be stomping in the mud, because it was worn by the killers of your fathers and brothers! The same mugs who shot me in '14, and who are sitting here laughing at you right now! With your effeminate gossip, your sickly flattery, your weak-kneed propaganda! This place is nothing but a suburb of the mass grave they've made out of Europe, and you're sitting here smiling about it like a bunch of mental patients!"

The meeting quickly dispersed, the collaborators anxiously filing out, white and funereal, the German officials murmuring to each other as they left the hall.

Among the latter group was Boemelburg, the S.S. boss. A German propaganda captain, obviously annoyed, came up and asked him about Céline.

"Who is this Frenchman who insults our uniform?"

"Ah, he's only a comic—none of it's serious! You know these French, always pulling your leg."

"I missed the joke," the propaganda captain said.

Boemelburg stared at him for a moment, registering the captain's displeasure, then dismissing it.

"I've read his books; the man's an artist, it's all in fun, quite harmless—he won't get out of hand like that again, I assure you. I know too many things about him. . . . There are certain things he's going to need from me. . . . Really, there's nothing to worry about. Just a little change of pace, all this, like an evening at the opera, good for the digestion!"

"Yes, I suppose." The *propagandastaffel* captain still sounded doubtful, but his grudging assent acknowledged Boemelburg's superior authority.

Vichy propaganda officers from the castle came to Céline's tiny room at the Löwen and suggested that, as the world-renowned author of the best-selling novels *Journey to the End of the Night* and *Death on the Installment Plan*—not to mention four popular anti-Communist and anti-Semitic pamphlets—he might help out with the war effort by producing articles or radio broadcasts. Céline glanced around to make sure there were no S.S. men listening, then laughed in the faces of these Frenchmen who remained committed to a lost cause—as if their commitment alone might spare them from the retribution he knew was coming.

"You must be joking! *I* help out? I've said it since '40: 'The Krauts are superfucked!' It's been obvious since then. German bones will be used as fertilizer for willow trees. And you may as well throw in the waltzes, the fantasias, the beer and the blood sausages. A lot of ugly mugs yelling 'Heil Hitler!' to the end. No, thank you, I don't care to be a valve on Goebbels' trumpet! 'The moon, green cheese . . .' And as to shilling for a packaged stucco socialism—of marshmallows and rutabagas!—No, I don't think so. I don't intend to become coal for Goering's fireplace or oil for his salad. I don't have the sensibility of a charcoal briquette!"

. . .

By midwinter Céline's recalcitrant attitude, and his willingness to express it, had earned him almost as many enemies inside Sigmaringen as out.

"It's like the scalding room in the slaughterhouse, here," he said to Chamoin one day as they were completing their fourth surgery in three hours. "The room where they scour the cattle before butchering them. Pass me that cotton, won't you? Really, Denmark looks better every day. I'd rather freeze than fry!"

"I don't know, doctor, perhaps you ought to reconsider Switzerland. Traveling to the north, it's far too dangerous."

"Norway, the North Pole! I don't care, Chamoin, as long as it's north! Scissors, please."

The doctor was bent over the supine body of a militiaman, cutting out a lipoma. He snipped slowly, severing the grayish mass, which was about the size of the top of a thumb, from the surrounding tissue. He removed it and placed it in a bottle of alcohol solution.

"He's not bleeding too badly, you see? Fine. Now we can sew him up. Pass that needle, will you? I hope it's sterilized."

The patient sat up and began to adjust his clothes over the bandage Chamoin had applied.

"The light in here is terrible," Céline said, washing up after the patient had left. "Really, it's lucky we aren't mutilating people."

"It's not luck, it's skill!"

"Thank you, my friend, but you're wrong. I'm a mediocre surgeon. Really, Chamoin, I have little talent for any of this. It's a vocation, that's all; I've got a vocation for medicine, but no gift for it. I had a gift for writing, you know, but no vocation. 'A writer'—the term makes you sick, doesn't it?"

Chamoin laughed. "But you're our best writer!"

"Our best fuckup! The champion at sticking his neck out! I stuck my head out the window into a hurricane. If I had known . . . but I lost, so I pay."

"Which of us knows at the beginning how it will all come out, doctor?"

Céline shook his head. "It was none of my business. All I had to do was shut up, not get on people's nerves, they'd have left me in peace."

Chamoin boiled water to clean the surgical tools.

Céline glanced up through the window at the complicated gingerbread stonework of the castle. When he turned back to his orderly, his eyes reflected his disquiet.

"What got me into it was curiosity. I was curious about things that were none of my business—Russia, the Jews. Curiosity cost me plenty. It got me involved with history. I thought I was going to make sense out of it all. In France now they say I'm crazy, you know, that I've got 'complexes.' Maybe they're right. My 'complex' is to fuck myself up by trying to make sense out of things. Nothing could be more arrogant. I was arrogant; I thought the problems of the world were going to get figured out in my lifetime, and all the great curves of experience were going to get completed right before my eyes—as if the whole thing was a spectacle cooked up just for me! Ah, I found out it doesn't work that way, Chamoin! One little life follows a certain curve, a very small one, but it belongs to a curve that goes far beyond us, and even leads out to the stars. That's fate. It carries us off like fleas in a squall. Our poor little trajectory is so small and feeble, like an old fellow's piss when he stands beside the Seine relieving himself. And yet we want to see the whole cosmic curve while we're still here." The doctor paused, smiled wearily at his orderly. "It's just not possible, Chamoin."

Young French soldiers of the militia, some on leave from the front, some without battle experience, came to Céline pleading to be certified unfit to return to action against the Russians. He signed false disability reports, even though there was a certain risk in it. He didn't see the point in sending more young men to die in Russia for Doriot and Hitler.

Jacques Doriot regularly visited the castle to recruit young men of the militia for the Charlemagne Brigade, French division of the Waffen S.S. This was the same Doriot who'd founded the L.V.F., the French force that fought with the Nazis in the snows of Russia.

Céline had changed his mind about Doriot. "Doriot is a man," he'd been saying in 1941. Then Doriot had come back from Russia, leaving behind him the bodies of thousands of dead Frenchmen. Doriot had a way of always landing on his feet, Céline noticed. An ex-Communist, later he'd been received at Berchtesgaden, with Ribbentrop and Himmler, who'd been ordered by the Führer to give Doriot all the support he needed. "You are a brave soldier," Hitler told Doriot, "I believe in your success." Out of this interview Doriot got a full staff, chauffeurs plus cars and gasoline, and his own newspaper. He was the chairman of the Committee for French Liberation at Sigmaringen. But he spent most of his time with his own private force, at Constance. In return for favors granted, he'd also become Hitler's principal talent scout among the French.

One night in February Doriot came to address the militia at Sigmaringen. To stir up prospective recruits, he spelled out his plans for recapturing France. He already had operatives at work, he said, running parachute drops and secret agents. He didn't mention that half his operatives died crossing the frontier. And the *Wehrmacht*, Doriot exclaimed, the *Wehrmacht* had incredible secret weapons! V-bombs from U-boats! Death clouds! Liquid-air rays! Atomic gases! The war could still be won!

After Doriot's proselytizing visit, Céline himself visited the militiamen's common room on a medical call.

It was a vast stone hall inside the castle, once a servants' refectory, now overcrowded with the field equipment and sleeping gear of a small battalion. On one wall there was a large battle map of Europe. A young militiaman, apparently affected by Doriot's speech, began asking Céline questions about the progress of the war; it was rumored among the militiamen that the doctor regularly received BBC reports from Paul Marion, one of the ministers. In reply Céline traced on the map the latest military developments. He indicated troop movements with gestures of his crippled right hand— its thumb and index finger locked together by paralysis to form a single spatulate digit.

"Look," he pointed, "Leclerc and his Africans are here in

Strasbourg. The Allies are up here in Metz. They've crossed the Rhine from the north, the Siegfried Line is *kaput*, see? The Russians, they're swarming in from the east. The white race is finished. The Boches, they tried to do the impossible here in the Ardennes; of course it didn't work, slowed things up by a month or so, that's all. Down here the Americans are coming across the Rhine from the south, into the Black Forest. Then here's the RAF, they're smashing things to pieces in all these cities"—he tapped the map at several points.

"And here at Ulm—you see how close it is! No houses left standing, they say. You've seen the people lining up outside the castle? There aren't enough food cards for them. Never will be. That's war for you. Only suckers go to war. I learned the hard way." He waved his crippled hand in the air. "You see? Flanders, '14—I know what I'm talking about. I found out what was up. It took me until the end; then I found out. The ones who hadn't gone to war had got rich; we who had gone were suckers. Oh, some of us became heroes. I had my mug on the cover of *National Illustrated*. But look at me now! And you, now you're being invited to become heroes. Dead faces in the mud. Not very heroic. Doriot is full of shit. Take it from me, this war is fucked . . ."

A heavy droning sound drowned out Céline's words. He stopped. He was shaking. No, the castle was shaking. He looked around and saw men scattering toward the exits. Planes were going over. . . .

. . .

Shortly afterward in a car on his way to Sigmaringen, where he was to meet with Déat, his rival among the ministers—perhaps to divide up shares in the future fascist France both still envisaged—Doriot was killed by a gunburst from an American plane. The ministers from Sigmaringen gathered to throw dirt on his grave in the snow—"and to shed crocodile tears," as Céline suggested privately to Lucette. "At least no more Frenchmen will be able to die for Doriot." He avoided the funeral.

Bombs hadn't yet fallen on Sigmaringen, but by now there were air-raid alerts nearly every night. It increased the habitual apprehensiveness of the doctor, whose nerves still jangled with echoes of the percussion of the Western Front in 1914.

Under the shadow of the castle, he studied escape routes as assiduously as he'd once written books. Now, however, instead of manuscript pages in sheaves held together by clothespins and hung on wires around his apartment, he had only handfuls of dashed hopes to show for his efforts.

The armies of Liberation were a drawstring closing on Sigmaringen. *Liberation* was a BBC term that now had a reverse significance for Céline. Language had a way of inverting, that dark winter—twisting inside out, like a building hit by a bomb. For Céline, "Liberation," as it was used on the radio, could mean one of three things—death at the hands of General Leclerc's allegedly bloodthirsty Africans; death at the hands of a vindictive summary court in Paris; or death at the hands of impromptu Resistance executioners. The latter fate, he was certain, was what would have been in store for him if he'd remained in France. "I'd never have seen the inside of the Court of Justice," he told Chamoin. "I got a tip. I was to be assassinated either at the Dental Institute or at the Villa Said."

The news from France supported his pessimism. Trials of collaborators were already going on. Most of them were swift and decisive. On February 6, 1945, the writer Robert Brasillach, a hired collaborator, Rebatet's colleague at *Je suis partout,* was executed. On March 16, the writer-collaborator Pierre Drieu la Rochelle, who faced the same sentence as Brasillach, took his own life.

"Death is just a cleaning machine," Céline had become fond of saying. Out toward the west you could sense it coming—a rumbling that on some nights at the castle seemed already audible.

Céline got to know the interior of the castle the way a burrowing rodent knows the tunnels of its home. It was a matter not of choice but of necessity. He constantly made calls there. These visits always made him uneasy. Who could say what horrors you might encounter in the depths of the castle? Its skyward turrets may have flown the French flag, but its innards, Céline knew, belonged to the principality of Death.

Wandering a sub-corridor on a medical errand one evening, he ran into a well-known assassin from Doriot's secret forces. The man was a veteran of the militant right-wing Action

Française. He'd tortured to death more than one captured member of the maquis, rumor had it; in underground circles his name reportedly struck terror. Before the war he'd functioned as a hired killer for the underworld. Now, Céline had heard, he was recruiting counter-Resistance workers for Doriot. He'd been seen around the castle, wearing an enigmatic smile but seldom saying a word.

This particular night he smiled at Céline as they passed each other in the darkened corridor. The smile was polite, almost deferential. Céline, who was carrying a candle, stopped dead in his tracks, feeling a mixture of fear and strong involuntary curiosity. He began to speak, but as he did so, his eye was caught by a large baroque ornamental mirror that hung from the corridor wall beside him. His image and that of the other man were captured momentarily on the glass. The candle Céline held out at shoulder height illuminated his own head but shaded his body, creating the freakish mirror-impression of a severed head floating in the dark. A final detail he'd been told about this fellow suddenly leaped into Céline's mind. The man was said to be an expert at garroting, having executed many people in that fashion . . . both on orders and on his own account.

Céline remained silent. The other man stared at him, still smiling. Céline brushed past and hurried down the corridor without looking back.

Through his black-market contacts, he got hold of a compass. In the Löwen, he discussed with Lucette their chances of making it over the snows into Switzerland on foot. Lucette would have no trouble. For Céline, at the age of fifty, ailing and quite a bit less athletic, it was a different story. The trip might be too much for him.

They went on talking and calculating. He pored over maps, gathered information on likely spots to cross the border. Rumors about the unfortunate experiences of others who'd tried the snow crossing made it seem less and less attractive. There were increasing numbers of border guards; police seemed the only thing not in shortage. Céline and Lucette set off on a practice voyage but turned back well short of the border when Bébert developed frozen paws.

Céline wouldn't be discouraged: Escape was now a mania with him. They tried another route, following a footpath one of the *passeurs* had described. The path skirted the edge of a lake. Picking their way through the snow, they were met by a sight that at first convinced Céline he'd lost his mind: The flat surface of the lake was suddenly broken by a head bobbing up from the depths, then another. Two naked men breast-stroked toward shore, laughing and talking in German. Céline rubbed his eyes with his mittens. Lucette, by his side, had already turned and begun to run back the way they'd come. Céline quickly followed. The Germans in the water hadn't noticed them. When Céline later interrogated the *passeur* who'd suggested the lake route to the frontier, the man explained that the Nazis had built a subterranean infirmary, with a sauna that issued into the lake.

"It's your bad luck that you went when you did," the *passeur* told Céline. "Perhaps another time . . ."

"The fellow must be crazy," Céline said to Lucette after he'd repeated this explanation. "Sending us past such a place! Boches who come up from the deep!"

The lake trip was Céline's last attempt to get out of Sigmaringen on foot. "We'll go the civilized way," he told Lucette. Behaving as naturally as possible and carrying no baggage, they went to the Sigmaringen station, pretending to be on a day trip, but in fact intending to cross the Swiss border by train. German soldiers turned them away at the station. The couple slunk sheepishly back to the Löwen.

Céline began writing letters to a Swiss lawyer, in hopes of getting a visa. The lawyer's application on his behalf was turned down, and anyway, the doctor lacked an exit pass out of Sigmaringen. He was, in effect, a German prisoner of war.

It was said that Brinon had been seen in Innsbruck, distractedly waiting in long lines at various consulates, trying unsuccessfully to get a visa. The diplomatic route appeared to be closed off.

There were other routes one heard discussed: Spain, for instance. Céline had friends there. But getting to Spain from Germany, that would take some doing. You had to get across the Alps to Merano, in the Italian Dolomites, and catch a plane from there. Ex-President Laval, who'd failed in attempts to get into Switzerland and Lichtenstein, and Abel Bonnard, the minister of education, got out that way. But theirs was the last plane out of Merano.

That left Denmark, Céline's first choice all along. Denmark

was where his gold was, the money from his books. In between, however, lay the black joke of Germany—Nosferatu with a bomb up his nose, ready to go off.

In March, Céline redoubled his efforts to escape to the north. He asked German friends to intervene with the Danish ambassador. This time his luck was better. The Danish government issued visas to him and Lucette. There remained the essential *ausweis*, exit pass out of Sigmaringen and permit for travel through Germany. Around Sigmaringen, such passes were as scarce as hope.

To obtain the *ausweis* Céline was forced to employ his professional expertise. Boemelburg had come to him about a urinary problem. Céline had relieved the condition by means of a prostate massage. The next time Boemelburg came to see him, he mentioned the *ausweis*. The S.S. boss replied with an enigmatic grunt. A week later he came to Céline's consulting room again.

Céline, wearing rubber gloves, massaged the S.S. chief's prostate. When it was over, Boemelburg pulled his pants up and winked at Chamoin. "I've seldom let Frenchmen put me in such a position," he said.

"Now remember," Céline told him, "noodles and water. No sex. Try to avoid alcohol, coffee and spicy foods."

Boemelburg, impassive, reached in his uniform jacket, pulled out three sets of exit visas and handed them to Céline. Céline studied them briefly, passed one on to Chamoin.

"As I said, Herr Sturmbahnführer, noodles and water! And absolutely no sex! If the urge comes over you, just imagine one of your dogs has just nipped you in the testicles. That'll take your mind off it!"

Boemelburg laughed softly. "And I've got some advice for *you*, doctor. Watch out for those Danish cops. They're not known for their sense of humor!"

2.
CHAOS

The March dusk
still came cold and early. In it a small group of collaborators
gathered again on the station platform, where they'd come
to greet Céline five months earlier. This time their numbers
had dwindled, as had their interest in conversation. Instead
of words their mouths produced brief puffs of white steam,
which floated off in the larger cloud of steam vented by the
little wood-burning engine that waited on a track from the
east.

Preparing to board the train, Céline, Lucette and Chamoin
stood together in a party of three, segregated from the others
on the platform not only by the baggage they carried but by

the accident of fate that had ordained they would have a chance at freedom, while the others stayed behind to face death or prison. It was as if these three had been released from gravity, given wings to escape while the others remained pressed to earth by the burden of history.

For Chamoin it was to be an illusory release. His travel papers stipulated that he accompany the doctor and his wife only as far as the Danish border, acting as their porter on the trip. He shouldered a sizable trunk that contained personal possessions the couple had salvaged in their exodus from Paris, then dragged across Germany in painful stages. In the trunk, among other items, were samples of Céline's mother's fine lacework, as well as several of his own manuscripts; with their thousands of pages of careful filigreed scribblings, these were fine lacework of another kind.

Lucette, the silent athlete, toted everything they'd need on the voyage—packed into sailors' bags, cloth slings and leather pouches, all hanging from a pair of bamboo poles balanced across her shoulders.

Céline himself carried a rucksack on his back. In the musette bag hung around his neck rode Bébert, the venerable tiger cat, who'd rebelled against Céline's decision to leave him behind in Sigmaringen. Consigned for adoption to a local shopkeeper, he'd escaped and found his way back to Céline and Lucette just as they were preparing to depart. Feeling guilty over attempting to leave him behind, Céline was relieved by Bébert's return and vowed never again to abandon him.

The doctor himself was bundled up in the same absurdly inflated costume now familiar to everyone at Sigmaringen: tattered battle jackets, mufflers and scarves. Over it all he'd donned a vast greatcoat into whose lining he'd stitched the syringe and a few ampules of morphine and cyanide—his last-ditch defenses against pain and life, respectively—along with some camphorated oil, a thermometer and his remaining gold coins.

The small locomotive hooted twice. Céline waved his coveted flag of escape, the *ausweis*, and beamed at the small crowd of collaborators on the platform. It was clear he felt no regrets about leaving. "We would not weigh heavily on his memory," Lucien Rebatet later said. The diminutive engine tottered out of the station, pulling one of Germany's last trains.

A few hours out of Sigmaringen, in the dark, the travelers reached the old city of Ulm, where they were told there were no trains departing until morning. Ever curious, Céline wanted to see what had become of the town. He didn't have to go far. Everything was flattened. Where there had once been houses, only blind facades remained. Two weeks had passed since the last raids. The ashes were cool.

The spectacle made Céline think of an experience he'd had in Hollywood. His fellow French writer Jacques Deval, who worked for a studio, had taken him for a tour of some sets. On one of them a historical drama about Pompeii was in production. Céline had been led through the set under a full moon. In bright moonlight, the ruins of Ulm now looked as unreal as that Hollywood Pompeii—eerie, spectral and somehow almost staged.

He grasped Germinal Chamoin's shoulder. It was a relief to feel the solidity of flesh under one's hand. "It reminds me of a movie set I once saw," he said. "People used to say, 'Life imitates art.' Crazy, eh, Chamoin? But now I'm starting to believe it. War imitates bad art, anyway, don't you think?"

Chamoin helped him climb over a fallen cornice. Beyond, the street they'd been walking down opened onto a broad avenue. On both sides all that remained of the dwellings were the facing walls, which loomed like studio false fronts.

Roasted down to calcium by phosphorus bombing, the ghostly, lunar-whitewashed ruins of Ulm did in fact resemble a movie set. Like extras waiting for a scene to be shot, a few stunned survivors of the flames milled around among the crumbled structures. Their clothes were dusted powdery white by ash. Both buildings and survivors looked as if some vindictive god had pounded them with angry fists, then coated the remains with lime. "It takes death to clean things up," Céline mumbled to Chamoin.

A badly burned man appeared out of the shadows and approached them, begging for a drink. Céline gave him water and an injection of morphine. The man told them the sky had been full of planes for days, that fires had burned everywhere; that once the chemical fire touched you, your body caught fire, nothing could put it out; and people who'd jumped into the Danube for relief had found that as soon as they'd emerged, their bodies once again burst into flames. "Tell me," the man moaned, tugging Céline's arm, "is it over? The war, I mean?"

The Ulm railroad station had been reduced to random atoms. There were tracks, but no building. Céline, Lucette and Chamoin huddled together in a cold makeshift barracks until dawn, then picked their way through the rubble of the city to New Ulm. There one platform was still standing. A train was waiting.

The hundred thousand tiny shocks produced by mile after mile of deteriorating tracks and bomb-plowed roadbed should have made sleep difficult. But the travelers were battling exhaustion. The shocks became hypnotic.

On such a voyage, sleep was merely another among many hazards. When you closed your eyes, it was in the knowledge you might never again open them. If death was coming, Céline preferred facing it. Bundled in woolens, sitting on the deck of a flatcar, he stared into the sky. Though at his side Lucette and Chamoin dozed, his own eyes remained open.

For Céline, keeping watch while others slept was almost second nature. He was used to living without sleep. It was a matter of training one's nerves, conserving as much strength as possible. He hadn't had a good night's sleep in over thirty years.

1914. A shell had blown up and thrown him against a tree. A small imbalance of air pressure for a half-second—and after all these years, his head was still full of the noises of invisible railroads, complete with whistles, brakes, pistons and bells.

It didn't matter whether or not you were actually on a train when you constantly had trains coming and going in your head! Shortly after the first injury, a German bullet had destroyed the radial nerve in his right arm, leaving him with chronic pain from shoulder to fingertip. On any given night—and particularly in times of stress—the two old injuries could be counted on to act up together, or in series; as soon as the auditory hallucinations abated, the nerve pain started up. As a consequence wakefulness had become a habit for him, much as reading or pipe smoking are habits for other people.

The train mysteriously jerked to a halt, venting steam. It took on some uniformed passengers who'd been waiting in the middle of a field, then slowly got under way again and labored north. Swaying in the uncertain grasp of a destiny it made no sense to try to understand, the doctor stared up into the sky.

The trains of 1945 were old, banged-up warhorses, relics from the days of the Kaisers. They ran on Germany's last supplies of low-grade fuel. The dying Third Reich could no longer afford to power its few remaining functional machines. The industrial might of the Ruhr was only a memory. The Reich had moved back in time. Once a mechanized wonder, these days it clanked along on the remnants of an obsolete nineteenth-century technology. Nobody knew for certain where or when the trains were running. There were inexplicable prolonged stops, re-routings, unexpected shuntings onto sidetracks while trains loaded with troops slowly rattled past.

At one point, while the travelers watched from a siding, a train full of British prisoners-of-war broke down on the main line. One prisoner tried to take advantage of the situation by escaping. Guards machine-gunned him alongside the right-of-way. A group of beggars who'd approached the halted train scattered at the sound of gunfire. As the train moved off, the beggars could be seen again, converging on the body of the fallen prisoner like hungry birds of prey.

It was a voyage that seemed as if it might go on forever. At times Céline imagined its true terminus as an imperceptible barrier. Once you stumbled over this thin barrier that separated the waking nightmare around you from the state of hallucination it so convincingly resembled, you came to the end of the voyage.

But meanwhile how could you remember where you were? Somewhere east of Ulm on the line to Augsburg—or beyond Augsburg, at Donauworth, just after crossing the river— Lucette spotted planes in the sky. Big four-engine bombers, a whole squadron! She pointed them out to Céline, who lay next to her amid their baggage on an open car crowded with refugees. "Not for us," he yelled over the sound of the train. "They've got better things to do, for the time being." The high, humming noise moved off.

Twenty minutes later the travelers felt a series of reverberating tremors like distant thunder, then heard a muffled, disrhythmic throbbing from the east.

"You see," said Céline. "They had business elsewhere."

"Munich?" Chamoin suggested. "The English?"

"No, Americans I think." Céline peered into the eastern sky, which began to glow with a faint orange light. The shocks continued. Gesticulating toward the horizon, he had to cry out to be heard over the combined train noise and distant explosions. "Or perhaps it's the Valkyries! The battle's over, they're dragging the dead bodies down the back steps of Valhalla!"

North was Céline's fixed idea. Huddled between Lucette and Chamoin on the open flatcar, he observed the sky with the rapt demeanor of a high priest studying celestial omens. Whenever the tracks veered to the left or right, he fretted until they curved back again toward the polar axis. Occupied with the sun and the stars, he appointed Chamoin to keep an eye on the rails. "Make sure we're going north, Chamoin! If the tracks turn east beyond those woods, it means we've been switched onto the Berlin line. That's no place for us!" The urgency of his injunctions might have tempted a visitor from another planet to suppose the train was actually being propelled not by its engineer but by Céline's orderly. "North, Chamoin, north! Don't let us stray from the Pole!"

. . .

Trains frequently stopped without warning. The doctor looked upon unexplained stops as a major cause for apprehension. A moving target at least had the advantage of movement. A stalled train was a sitting duck. If the delay lasted more than a few minutes, he clambered down to investigate the situation. Hobbling along at trackside on two canes, his stooped, swinging gait exaggerated the simian posture often commented on by those who'd met him in recent years. "I don't mind being called an ape," he'd once remarked, "as long as they don't go a step further with their insults and call me a man!" The German trainmen and conductors he pestered with his endless questions began calling him *"Der affe"*—"the monkey."

There were long delays in open countryside. Guards came up and down the length of the train, checking papers. The weather was very cold. With paralytically stiff hands, you fumbled through your things until the papers were found, then presented them with whatever alacrity could be summoned, prepared for the worst.

It was almost possible for the travelers to envy the labor gangs who toiled at repairing bomb-damaged sections of track. The gang hands at least managed to work up a sweat even when it was freezing. The gangs were a sight to behold: the last dregs of the German work force. A few old men and boys, many women, ample numbers of the sick and wounded, dressed in dirty bandages and rags piled over rags. Their faces wore expressions of numbed grief, beyond despair.

At one way station south of Nuremberg a gang of track workers pressed in around the train. With their hands to their mouths they made smoking gestures, sucking obscenely at their frostbitten fingers to solicit the travelers for cigarettes. Céline, who didn't smoke, was carrying a few packs of black-market cigarettes as currency. He tossed one to a pregnant woman whose face was smeared with soot. She stood mesmerized, watching the pack land in the frozen mud, and didn't move until several grubby boys saw it and made for it. Then, throwing down her shovel, she snatched it up. One of the boys tore it out of her hands and started to run. A guard blocked his path. When the guard pulled a pistol out of his holster, the boy stopped abruptly and dropped the pack at his feet. Bending at the knees while pointing his gun at the boy, the guard stooped to pick it up and pocketed it.

"Merde!" Céline turned away in disgust and climbed back on the train. As they pulled out, he saw the pregnant woman still standing along the tracks. She was looking at him with the empty gaze of an automaton.

The farther north they went, the more planes they saw. Allied bombers droned overhead continuously. At night the travelers beheld flashes of bright color on the horizon, then heard a low rumbling. Cities were drowning in fire somewhere. The RAF was at work. The English pilots were the gods of the night sky, bringing thunderbolts that made the earth burn in the distance.

By day there were American planes, and their pilots were watchful. Now and then one of them picked out the smoke of the train, whose wood-burning engine gushed thick black puffs that served as an unmistakable lure. If the plane was part of a whole squadron, it usually had somewhere else to go. Stray planes, however, were much more likely to take an interest. Now and then one would wiggle its wings, veer out of its flight pattern and wheel back around to come in on a trajectory parallel with the tracks.

First you heard a thin, high-pitched whining sound, which quickly grew into a screaming whistle. The sky lit up, the earth trembled, dirt flew, the air got dark as if with storms. Then the train eased to a slow crawl; you dove down the slope of the embankment into an open ditch, covered your head with your hands. The hot whirlwind came closer, even touched you: Were those things hitting your back and shoulders mere pebbles and clods of dirt, or were they fragments of metal cutting into your flesh?

The planes went by, and you came back to consciousness, your mouth as dry as cotton, your heart pounding like a piston at the top of your throat. You realized you were lying in a cold pile of dirty snow; tears were running down your face; your hands were shaking. You got back on the train.

The daylight raids compressed time into fused moments of terror and panic. But bad as the days were, the nights made you yearn for the days. The nights were the longest part of the journey.

There was one night that didn't end but kept on going all through the next day. Shortly before dawn the train attracted a small bomber patrol group just as it was approaching a tunnel. Bombs began to fall. The engineer made a run for the tunnel at full throttle, then once inside immediately applied his brakes. The train shuddered to a stop, with only the locomotive poking out at the other end—where it had to remain to prevent asphyxiation of the passengers.

Dawn broke. Like bees drawn to nectar, the bomber pilots came back to see if the train had emerged. As bombs thundered down on the earth above, the travelers cowered helplessly in pitch-darkness, stones and gravel raining on them. Overhead, the timbers of the tunnel shook. Fearful the roof beams and supports would collapse, the passengers finally crawled under the carriages. Lying on his belly, his mouth full of cinders, Céline railed and cursed into the dark. "Blind sadists! Fuckers of the dead! Drunk on revenge! Go on, then! Go on, blow the whole mountain to kingdom come!"

Not until night came on again did the train finally begin to move.

There were no schedules, no timetables. Picking an itinerary out of this chaos was a matter of following your instincts. But that was Céline's specialty. Once, acting on a hunch he couldn't explain, he chose one train over another when both were leaving at nearly the same time for the same destination, by diverging routes. At the next station he learned the other train had been destroyed in a bombing raid.

The travelers crossed Nuremberg on foot by night, in the midst of heavy RAF incendiary bombing. The decimated center of the city was a new circle of hell. Wounded women and children wandered through the rubble in a daze. Now and then flares fell, the sky ripped open, fallen angels rose again only to expire in a fiery shower. The travelers walked through a night rent by fluttering sparks and sudden phosphorescent cascades.

Now Céline pulled himself forward on one cane; the other was lost. Leaning on Lucette, he cried into the incandescent night—"Fucked, this world is fucked! It's over!" Lucette consoled him, told him they hadn't far to go, soon the worst of it would be behind them. His shouting tapered off into a muttered stream of insults, directed this time not to the bomber pilots but into a malign universe beyond.

Chamoin trundled their baggage over the smashed cobblestones on a wheelbarrow. The pulverized ruins were hot enough to blister the soles of their feet even through leather boots. Waves of heat twisted the ends of their eyebrows into small burned curls. Squinting through the smoke, they passed the remains of the great arena, where Hitler had reviewed the *Wehrmacht* in its glory. At last they came to a shunting yard beyond the town walls. There a crowd of refugees was awaiting the northbound train.

After Nuremberg, it was hard to keep track of possessions. What they managed to hang on to were those things they kept closest to their bodies—their travel papers, the little food they had left: some rice and flour, potatoes, tea. The luggage got lighter and lighter. This or that item would disappear: Lucette's castanets, her collection of Indian jewelry. Particular losses had no meaning; they quickly merged into a general sea of loss. The train rattled on.

North through Furth to Erlangen . . . Bamberg . . . Outside Bamberg, at an impromptu stop caused by track damage, there was a stream with fresh water. Water of any kind was hard to find; clean water was a revelation. They drank, then washed for the first time in days. Someone had made a fire by trackside. Lucette fished out of her bag a small metal teapot she'd brought from Paris, made tea and served it to a crowd of their fellow travelers.

Almost all of them were refugees. Most were heading north in hopes of getting to Denmark or Sweden—or anywhere that wasn't on fire. Many were children with no families left. They stared wide-eyed at everything. Others were sick or injured. Céline did what he could for those who seemed worst off, using his last medicines and bandages. Finally he was reduced to improvising dressings out of rags. Giddy with exhaustion, he bent to examine anyone who could no longer stand up. When Lucette begged him to rest, he waved her away.

"There's an Italian fellow over there who's going to Finland for some reason. How do you explain that, Luci? Probably there's no reason at all; he's simply out of his head. He's got second-degree burns, a fractured tibia and he expects me to get him to Finland! How can I rest, Luci? These people expect miracles. I can't perform miracles. What's needed is morphine and cemeteries."

"You should go over by the fire and lie down."

"It's too late to talk about 'should,' Luci. If it's a matter of 'should,' we had our chance! We should never have left Montmartre. We should have shot ourselves. Yes, that would have been the only decent way out of all this!"

Back and forth between destroyed stations, in a slow zigzag through the inferno, they gradually made their way north. They passed smashed trains, abandoned fields, barren farms, dikes and silos gouged out of the ground, frozen carcasses of dogs and plowhorses, a Bruegel landscape brought up to date by modern war.

The university town of Göttingen had gone virtually untouched by the bombing that leveled surrounding cities. Did that mean the gods of vengeance respected scholarship? In the station Lucette discovered a woman who had bread to trade. She gave the woman a pair of jade earrings for three loaves, then spread a cloth on the concrete floor of the station and divided the bread with other refugees they'd met on the train. Some of the others also had food to contribute. There was half a tin of ham put in by a Lithuanian worker, who said he was on the run from a Nazi war plant and trying to get back to his family. A skinny, gimp-legged Pole produced some sausage and a rind of cheese out of a greasy, well-traveled rucksack.

Céline gave his share of the sausage to Bébert.

"Your cat is fat enough to make somebody a fine meal," the Pole said, observing Bébert with an eye obviously trained in the economics of hunger. "A cat like that would be worth . . . oh, say, a pound of flour and a cup of sugar."

"He's not for trade," Céline said firmly.

The little party of refugees was camped under the station clock, which had evidently stopped some time past. Its hands pointed to the wrong Gothic numerals. The Pole gazed up at the clock, a sardonic smile wrinkling the corners of his wide, thin-lipped mouth. "In a few days you might start whistling a different tune."

South of Hanover their train ran into visual range of an American bomber wing. Minutes later the tracks were hemmed in by explosions. A nearby burst knocked Lucette off their open car, throwing her completely clear of the slowly moving train and onto the gravel embankment. Bébert, in his musette bag, was also thrown from the train. Céline scrambled down and ran to them. Bébert had landed on his feet and was uninjured. Lucette was less fortunate. She jumped up to show Céline there was nothing to worry about, then fell back down again, one knee giving out under her. The knee had been sprained in her sudden landing on the embankment.

The bombers were gone as quickly as they'd come. They'd managed to hit the locomotive, however. It was now a twisted jumble of smoking metal at the front of the train. Several cars were derailed. Worse, the travelers saw sections of torn-up track coiling into the air like snakes from a charmer's box. Even with a new locomotive, the train couldn't be moved until the tracks were fixed. Hanover, a dimly pulsing glow on the horizon, was still several miles off.

Céline examined Lucette's knee. It was swollen and bruised,

but there was no fracture. She insisted she could walk. He fashioned a brace by wrapping a scarf around her knee, and they set off on foot. Now at least there was less baggage to carry. The bomb blast had blown one of their bags off the train, and most of its contents had been broken or scattered along the tracks. It was no time to worry about lost possessions. Chamoin hauled the heavy trunk on his shoulders until his legs faltered under the weight. Then the Lithuanian, who'd been with them since Göttingen, took a turn carrying it. Out in front of the ragtag procession Lucette limped along gamely at Céline's side. The Pole wobbled behind, favoring his own bad leg.

"You see," Céline said to Lucette, "I've become the pied piper of the lame and the halt!"

It seemed hardly an exaggeration. Other refugees stranded by the bombing and derailment joined their group as they walked. Following at a distance of ten or fifteen yards was a small gang of starved-looking children who tagged along like flies on a fruit truck, hoping to be fed. At the head of the children was an elderly English couple who seemed to have appeared out of nowhere. Slowed by a crippled hip, the Englishman couldn't walk very well. In any other group of hikers he'd have had trouble keeping up, but not in this one.

When the Englishman found that Céline spoke his language, he began a conversation. Like many refugees, he had a story to tell. He'd been keeping horses at an estate in the German countryside, he said, until bombs started landing on it.

As they walked along, Céline translated the Englishman's

story for Lucette and Chamoin. "It sounds fishy," he said in French. "On the other hand, nobody would be in this situation unless he was as desperate as us, would he? Who cares what his reasons are?"

"Maybe the guy's a spy," suggested Chamoin.

"Why would a spy have his wife with him?" Lucette smiled at the Englishman's wife. A small woman, weighed down by two big suitcases, she smiled back politely but said nothing.

Between turns carrying Céline's trunk, the Lithuanian helped the English couple with their bags. He was a fair-haired, stony-faced man of about thirty, with pale brows. His light blue eyes appeared as flat and unblinking as those of ancient statues. He too had a story to tell as they hiked along. Speaking in halting German, he said that his home was in Vilna, where he'd been a woodworker until the Russians took over his country. They'd sent him off to fight in the Red Army. His unit had been captured by the Germans. Most of his fellow soldiers had been shipped to concentration camps, but he'd been sent to a German airplane factory. The RAF had made short work of the factory. He was now hoping to make it back across Russian lines to his home.

"This fellow's even crazier than us, Luci," Céline said to his wife after hearing the man's story. "He wants to go to the East!" He turned to the Lithuanian. "You'll never make it."

"I've got papers," the man said.

"Forged, I take it?"

The Lithuanian nodded. "But they're very well done."

"So are mine, but I wouldn't try to get across the eastern front with them. Over there—" Céline hesitated, pausing to lean on his cane and look the man in the eye—"if either side catches you, you're fucked."

"Yes," the Lithuanian said impassively. "I don't ever expect to see my home again."

"In that you have something in common with us all."

The grim little party stumbled along, following the tracks.

There was a low pounding noise coming out of the north. Quick flashes of light danced along the deepening Prussian-blue band of the northern horizon. The air in that direction seemed charged, as if with static electricity. It was a setting for the opening movement of a Bruckner symphony, full of melodramatic foreboding. That was Hanover, dead ahead.

They came upon a ghostlike figure crawling along the tracks, a rough bundle of shadows dressed in the field gray of a German officer. As gray as the cold, muddy gravel of the roadbed, the crawling ghost had a bag slung over its shoulder.

They moved closer. *"Guten abend,"* the ghost said without looking up. *"Guten abend,"* said Céline. Stirring the mud with one hand, the ghost fished up a spent shell cartridge and deposited it in the bag. *"Kupfer,"* the ghost said, twisting around to smile up at them through broken teeth.

"Copper!" Céline turned to Lucette and Chamoin. "The fellow's doing a little independent salvage work, that's all!"

The ghost's hand went back into the bag, pulled up something wrapped in tinfoil and held it out. *"Chokolade!"* It was a bar of English chocolate. Where would such a thing come from? The smiling ghost explained with a combination of words and a few expressive gestures: an English plane, no bombs, but chocolate. Why? The ghost shrugged. Some things couldn't be understood, much less explained.

Céline exploded into laughter. "Chocolate falling from the sky!"

The Pole stepped forward and offered the ghost a cigarette. *"Rauchen sie Juno, eh?"*

"Juno?" The ghost beamed. *"Ja, ja."*

The Pole struck a match. Down in the mud, the ghost puffed and grinned, waved the chocolate bar, pointed to their bags, made eating motions. Lucette pulled out a potato and a crust of dry black bread, handed them to the ghost.

"Danke, danke!" The ghost nodded appreciatively and gave her the chocolate.

The travelers started to go, but the ghost called out after them. "Hanover?" With a puzzled frown the ghost pointed a bony finger off in the direction of the burning city. Céline glanced at the others. "He thinks we're out of our heads, going to Hanover."

"Perhaps he's got a point," the Pole said.

They set out again, nibbling the sky-fallen chocolate as they walked. It was getting dark; the tracks were hard to follow. But orange and green flames, swirling low in the sky before them, made Hanover easy to find.

.   .   .

As a full moon climbed in the clear, chill sky, stars gradually appeared overhead, glittering on the body of the night like the scales of a huge beached fish. An occasional cloud drifted by, its underside rosy with reflections of the flames ahead.

South of the city there were ambulance and troop trains stalled on the main line. A guard with a machine gun halted the travelers. "No more civilian trains on this stretch," he said. "If you really want to go to Hanover, you'll have to get there on foot." At this, the crippled Englishman suddenly broke into tears. He was simply too tired to go on, his wife explained. "We need a rest anyway," Céline said. Chamoin went off to scout the tracks ahead.

Plans were debated. The Pole suggested abandoning the Englishman if he couldn't continue. But Chamoin returned with a baggage cart he'd found. He loaded Céline's trunk aboard, then helped the Englishman and Lucette struggle up alongside it. Bent almost double, his face lined with strain and the veins of his neck bulging, Chamoin lurched forward, hauling the loaded cart along the gravel embankment. Céline, on his cane, swung along ahead, keeping an eye out for whatever might be coming. They passed through the suburbs.

The ruins of Hanover were still ablaze. Eighty percent destroyed, the city continued to burn, fed by the phosphorus and thermite of the RAF. Flames still fluttered over the flattened houses, chemical butterflies with pink and orange wings. The travelers had to improvise a path between two rows of caved-in buildings. Yellow and green wraiths of fire popped suddenly out of fragmentary doorways, like gas jets jumping from burner to burner at random across a vast stove.

The air was thick with a dense hot fog. To keep from inhaling burning particles they stretched handkerchiefs over their faces. It was very slow going. In fact, crossing Hanover as it burned was a feat the travelers might have accomplished more swiftly had they been circus firewalkers. As it was, the agile and tireless Chamoin showed himself to be a true acrobat of chaos. Prying open invisible cracks in walls of smoking wreckage, he squeezed himself through, and then, after investigating, came back to escort the others.

They passed a young woman who was staggering around in a fresh bomb crater, holding a baby in one arm. The woman had her black shawl pulled up around her mouth so as not to breathe smoke. She was singing as she wandered through the rubble. *"In der nacht ist der mensch nicht gern allein . . ."* Her face and hands were badly burned. As the travelers watched, she tripped and fell, the baby pitching forward out of her arms.

Startled, Lucette cried out. The Pole and the Lithuanian, who were closest to the crater, ran forward to help the fallen woman. But just as they got to the lip of the crater, she climbed to her feet again, clutching the baby. She stared at them. In her eyes hatred flashed out. "It's too late," she wailed. "This child is dead!"

It had been a long, broad residential street. If it were ever to become that again, future generations would have their work cut out. They'd have to rebuild from the ground up. As for the street's inhabitants, it looked as if new ones were going to have to be found. The people who'd been living here when the bombs came down obviously weren't going to need housing anymore.

On both sides of the street the skeletons of buildings were still burning. There were signs that the rain of fire from the air had taken the street by surprise. The travelers passed several men in army uniforms. The men stood against intact sections of wall, stiff and still as statues in the moonlight. Phosphorus clung like cake icing to their bodies. Caught in a grotesque diorama of death, these corpses of Hanover had been spun into a permanent cocoon of flame.

Two young men ran past. Boys, really—about fifteen or sixteen. They were soldiers, apparently. Their quasi-military costumes made it hard to tell. They wore women's underclothing, one suit of it over another, with leggings of coiled newspapers stuffed into high paratroop boots and German army helmets several sizes too large. They ran ahead, across the leveled building sites. They did ballet leaps over flames that shot up as if from a concealed blowtorch. Now and then one of them disappeared into the shadows, then emerged with some prize. A sausage, a jar of jam, a tin of powdered milk. Fire leaped up around them. Their youthful faces back-lit by the flames, they looked like figures out of some medieval allegory, representing Fear and Manic Hunger.

A little farther on they came to a spot where a block of apartment buildings had once stood. Thin pink and violet flames still spiraled up out of the embers of the building foundations. In a cleared area at the center of the ruins a pack of unkempt women had a fire going. They were banqueting, their haggard faces livid in the moonlight.

"The witches of Macbeth!" Céline exclaimed. "They fit right in, don't they?" He incanted a few lines in English, drawing out the vowels for effect. " 'Now o'er the one half world Nature seems dead!' "

The women were busy cooking the body of a horse. While two of them tended the fire, the others poked at the flesh of the slowly roasting animal, ripping off pieces and eating them with their hands.

Chamoin's cart had been abandoned. Lucette and the Englishman were walking again. The Englishman kept falling down. When he smelled the cooking meat, he took a few wavering steps in the direction of the women's campfire. "Perhaps they'll feed us," he said.

"Don't go near them." Céline waved his cane. "Those gangs of whores can be as deadly as wolf packs. I've seen them in Prussia. They won't stop at horses, either. They're capable of devouring old men!"

The Englishman started to cry again.

Céline was nearing his own limits of exhaustion. Things around him had begun to wobble when he looked at them. He shut his eyes. From one step to the next he started to topple. He planted his cane, but it did no good. He continued to sag toward the pavement. Chamoin ran to him, caught him before he fell.

"We've got to stop and rest," Lucette said.

Beyond the residential block there was a park. Trees surrounded a little lake. Bombs had landed there also. The lake was now a deep crater. Some tall willows and poplars had been turned into strange twisted charcoal sculptures. The travelers lay down on the scorched grass. As the eastern sky began to lighten, the last wash of moonlight bathed everything in terrible clarity. All around the park the travelers could see rooms of houses that had been peeled open by bombs. The rooms had the artificial drama of department-store window displays. The growing daylight revealed cobwebby, asphalt-encased tablefuls of food laid out for meals never eaten. The residents had fled from their dinner tables into eternity.

The sun floated up over the jagged shell of the city and hung low in the sky like a lemon on a plate of dry ice. The travelers were too weary to move. The Pole and the Lithuanian huddled together. Finally the Pole got up and walked over to where Céline was lying. "We're taking off for the East," he said.

"All right," Céline said.

"Perhaps we'll meet again."

"I don't think so."

A dog howled somewhere in the ruins.

The light of day in Hanover was a smoky yellow haze. The rail line across the city had been destroyed. At the Hanover-South depot they found a crowd of the homeless and wounded, no trains, not even any military guards. A Red Cross tent had been set up. There was water and a cooking fire. Lucette made tea in canvas buckets, boiled their last potatoes and grains of rice.

They went on to the Hanover-North station, where a state of confusion reigned. It was hard to find out anything about the movements of trains. Rumor held that there would be no more trains going north: All the lines were damaged, all the locomotives out of service. An unexploded bomb suddenly went off in a building near the station, creating panic among the refugees. Women and children wailed, old men held their heads in their hands. Outside, the bells of fire crews could be heard, moving around the ghost city.

Then, around noon, a train unexpectedly came in. The word quickly spread: a shipment of war matériel for the north! "Anything to keep the killing going a few more hours," Céline said. "A few hundred more dead men, for what?" He, Lucette and Chamoin joined the throng of travelers pushing toward the train.

The train was made up of open cars carrying big yellow searchlights, spools of cable, dynamos, transformers. Jostled by the crowd, the travelers scrambled aboard the first car that wasn't already overloaded. Céline wedged himself under the big glass eye of a searchlight, pulling Lucette in behind him. Chamoin took out a knife and cut large swatches from the tarpaulins that covered the heavy equipment. Wrapping the tarp cuttings around themselves like capes, they curled up to wait for the train to move.

Other refugees climbed aboard. The English couple was out of sight, maybe on another car? Chamoin jumped down, searched the train for them. They weren't to be found. This trip was like that. People came into your life out of nowhere, then disappeared again. You couldn't be sure later if they'd really existed at all.

Under a pale distant sun the train inched out into the Saxon countryside. It was poor farmland, hard, cold and featureless. For the first ten kilometers or so the tracks were in very bad shape. The train halted repeatedly. Deadbeat work crews loitered along the embankments. Old women in layers of wool underwear slowly pounded at the frozen gravel with picks and shovels. Once when the train slowed down, a wild-eyed soldier with a huge bandage around his head came out of a field and began running alongside, waving his arms and hollering unintelligible phrases at the refugees on the open cars. Watching him, Céline broke out in bitter laughter. "The German army is providing us with an escort!"

After an hour or so the track condition improved. The train picked up speed. Snow was starting to fall, first in light flurries, then thicker flakes. The shivering travelers huddled closer together. The wind blew snow in their mouths and eyes. Tears froze on their faces.

When Céline closed his eyes, colors swirled in circles, then went white. He wasn't sure anymore whether he was really seeing what he thought he was seeing. As they went through Luneberg, where bombs had created a bizarre new landscape, he thought he saw a locomotive perched on top of a pile of scrap iron. He sat up, startled. Contradicting the laws of man was one thing, but contradicting the laws of nature—*merde*! When the implausible became the probable, anything at all was possible—even the most ridiculous visions!

But it was no vision. The locomotive was really there. It had been tossed into the air by the impact of a direct hit. Céline's eyes bulged out in amazement. Unshaven, sleepless, lightheaded and experiencing a powerful sense of dissociation and displacement, he wore the baleful look of a man who in a few nights and days had witnessed an entire millennium of evil. Snow dusted his face. He pulled the tarp down over it.

The old coke engine that was pulling their train broke down twice but finally got them as far as the port district of Hamburg. There, in the mud of the harbor, they saw big boats turned upside down by the recent RAF night bombing. The keels pointed skyward like kids' toys left in the sand. Cranes, docks, warehouses and the rest of the harbor structures had been blown completely away. The port now consisted of several square miles of twisted steel, powdered stone and boats upside down in mud.

Wings black with pitch and coal tar from the fires along the Elbe, gulls wheeled overhead. The gray sky leaked snow that turned to steam before it landed. Yellow puddles collected on the ground, some of them simmering like miniature geysers.

Céline, Lucette and Chamoin hiked north from the port. They passed through the Sankt-Pauli district. Before the firestorms Sankt-Pauli had been famous for its night life. The only night life now was the life of ghosts. A blue mist hung in the air. The omnipresent odor of hot tar at first made Céline think of roadwork. No matter how hard you tried to imagine that this smell was no different than the odor of tar around a road repair site on a hot day in France, you couldn't ignore a secondary odor that clung to the tar smell. It was an aroma like that of roast pork, but it wasn't coming from some out-of-the-way restaurant or street vendor. Bodies and body parts, some burned black, some still pink as salmon or the worms you'd find in the wet grass of a spring morning, lay scattered through the fine pumicelike dust of the ruins. The stench was nauseating.

Particularly so for Lucette. She'd once visited Hamburg for several weeks with a touring dance company. She told Céline she couldn't put out of her mind the faces of people who'd been sitting in the audience as she'd performed. "They might be under our feet right now," she said.

Looking for the railroad station, the travelers came to an inverted bomb crater shaped like an earth mound. They stopped and walked around this strange dome of rubble. It was an enormous blisterlike bell of clay pockmarked with extruded polyps of brick and glass. Through gaps in the toppled masonry you could stick your head in and look around. Parts of the building foundation and structural timbers were still intact. In the dome's igloolike interior the travelers could make out whole bodies rolled up in membranes of liquid asphalt. Packages were strewn around.

It had once been a grocer's shop. It wasn't hard to deduce what had happened to it. A bomb had landed. The shop had imploded into itself. The grocer still sat at his counter, as lifelike in his lacquer suit of phosphorus as any exhibit in a wax museum. The travelers took turns peeping in at him through the gaps. "The bomb caught him short," Céline said. "He was still counting his money."

Chamoin squeezed inside the dome. Ignoring Céline's anxious warnings, Lucette crawled in behind. Céline kept an eye on them through a hole, voicing his fears that the dome might collapse on them at any moment. "Be careful, Lucette! Watch out for that knee of yours!" Finally Lucette and Chamoin emerged—coughing and covered with soot, but carrying packages of canned fish, ham, biscuits, dried milk. As if drawn to food by some sixth sense that inspires the hungry, a flock of ragamuffins charged out of the surrounding ruins. The travelers divided their booty with these orphans of the flames. For once there was enough food to go around. Bébert, always favored by Céline, got three tins of sardines to himself.

Over the city of Hamburg the smoke floated in black, sulfurous bands. This permanent pall blocked out much of the sun's light. There was anyway not much left to see. The only intact structures were the huge reinforced concrete ack-ack fortresses, which looked like medieval castles except for the guns bristling from multiple turrets. As they passed under one of these antiaircraft fortresses, Céline cast a derisive glance up toward its gun turrets. He poked his cane skyward. "Architecture of the future!" The towers crouched over the ruins like giant frogs on a pond of dust. Soot-blackened seagulls sailed around the turrets. Now and then a gunner fired a few errant rounds at them, but the gulls didn't seem to notice.

Where the fires had ceased to burn, the devastated city had turned white: Here falling snow didn't become steam but settled onto the ashes like a wedding gown landing on exposed bone. Flakes clung to the travelers' clothes. With scarves wrapped over their faces to block out the cold wind that carried fumes of decomposing flesh, they resembled bedouins crossing the Sahara, slowly merging with the powdery whiteness of the calcined debris around them. It snowed harder. All around there were white bundles. Maybe they were corpses. After a while it was hard to tell the living bundles from the dead ones, except that if you watched long enough the living ones moved.

They came to a relief station. A canopy had been stretched across the empty shell of a smashed house. Under it, at a picnic table, a few forlorn figures sat hunched over tin mugs. There was a fire. A first-aid warden was in charge.

The warden struck up a conversation with Céline. The caged animals from the Hamburg zoo had broken loose in the bombing, the warden said. Burned by phosphorus, wounded or in shock, they'd reverted to a wild state, roaming the ruins in search of food and water. Bears, stags and elephants had been seen on the streets.

"You saw all this?" asked Céline.

The warden grinned. There was relish in his voice. "I saw an ape sitting in a bomb crater, drinking a bottle of ink."

Céline shook his head in disgust. "The suffering of animals in war is something only a cretin could find funny."

"And how is it worse than our own?"

"They're at least innocent, aren't they?"

The defiance in Céline's tone made the warden eye him suspiciously. "This particular ape didn't look innocent at all. He had a lot of blood caked in his fur, and burns and a very nasty look on his face. I wouldn't have gone near him, I can assure you." Planting a blunt finger in the middle of Céline's chest, the warden raised his voice. "Besides, what's one gorilla more or less when people are dying all over the place?"

Céline stepped back. "Men deserve what they get in war," he said coldly, "absurd and destructive gorillas that they are!" He turned to Lucette and Chamoin. "This place is full of lunatics!" Putting down their tin mugs, they followed him out of the shelter.

The roof of the Hamburg station was gone. A single platform stood at one end of the pulverized depot. Refugees had set up camp there. Around midnight there'd be a train going north, it was claimed. Céline waited with his wife and orderly under a sky swept by blue and white beams of huge searchlights. The beams illuminated only an occasional eel-shaped cloud. "A fairy tale!" Chamoin said.

"Yes," said Céline, "but one in which the spirits of the air carry death in their wings instead of magic!"

Just before midnight, the beams picked out a fleet of Lancasters. They passed directly over the station, moving south. The travelers waited, listening to the bombing going on in other parts of the city, then to the bells of the fire brigade. Finally a train came in. Another antique wood-burner, the locomotive looked as if it belonged in a history book.

It pulled out, groaning its way through the yards. The travelers had secured places on a flatcar, under some large, unrecognizable piece of equipment. Maybe a gun armature? It didn't matter; they were too tired to care. Night and cold closed in. They huddled together, sinking into the slow, regular rhythm of the train.

Late at night they reached the Kiel Canal. A policeman in Hamburg had told Céline the canal had taken heavy bombing every night for the past two weeks. This night proved no exception.

Along the canal the train made several prolonged stops for no apparent reason. Down steep banks to one side you could see water moving, and blinking lights: a string of U-boats idling, waiting for permission to enter the North Sea. "This is their gullet," Céline told Chamoin. "The North Sea is the mouth, the Baltic is the belly. Hitting them here is like cutting their windpipe. The British know all that; they're as precise about destruction as any surgeon!"

Chamoin rolled his eyes and smiled. "I hope they'll at least wait until the night's swallowed us up!"

Minutes later an RAF squadron came over. The planes dropped magnesium flares that fell in blue, fanlike rivers, lighting up the lacework of iron arches and girders in the footbridges that spanned the canal. "Look at those bridges!" Céline marveled. "They'd come up to the first story of the Eiffel Tower!"

Up ahead, a bomb went off, then another. The footbridges

shook like dollhouses. The travelers scrambled down and took cover beside the train. The blasts started to move down the embankment toward them.

Céline rolled over Lucette to shelter her. "I told you it would come to this, Luci!" he shouted over the noise of the approaching explosions. "We should never have left Paris! There at least we could have died without so much trouble! Dying like this is fucked!"

The bridges and ramparts ahead, where the railway crossed the canal, were lit up clearly by more flares—a bouquet of red, yellow and violet blossoms. Just as they started to wilt and droop, more bombs hit, flooding the night with brilliant corollas of fire. The bridges groaned as if their superstructures were ready to crack.

Somewhere toward the front of the train there was a man hollering in a language Céline couldn't make out.

"This flower bombing, it leaves you blind and deaf at once," he yelled to Chamoin. Chamoin was yelling something back. Céline only saw the "O" his mouth made.

Finally the flares stopped falling and darkness came back. The night was quiet. Now it was just a matter of waiting for morning.

The train moved out after dawn, crossed the precariously swaying bridges, then rolled over an empty winter landscape of broad plains, dull yellow fields with claylike stains underneath. An hour, two hours of nothing. Finally there were a few farmhouses. From the car in front of theirs a soldier in uniform shouted back, "Flensburg! End of the line!"

At the Flensburg station the travelers saw the Danish flag, red with a white cross, flying next to the Nazi banner. On the pavement outside the station hundreds of refugees had gathered. They moved around constantly, trying to keep warm. German guards, holding submachine guns, patrolled the perimeter of the crowd, like doleful shepherds tending a disconsolate flock.

Inside the station there were more refugees, jamming the waiting room and spilling over onto the platforms.

Everybody was waiting for the same thing, the first train heading north across the border. Everybody, that is, except Germinal Chamoin. Chamoin was to take the first train back into Germany. Céline had leaned heavily on Chamoin's services all through the trip. Now at the end of it, coming off the train at Flensburg, the doctor's legs folded under him; he dropped his cane and found himself lying on the concrete. He couldn't walk anymore, that was all there was to it. Chamoin picked him up and carried him into the station like a sack of laundry.

Céline seemed to be wandering in and out of a state of shock. When it struck him that they were really losing Chamoin, he fumbled through the pockets of his aviator's jackets and came up with their remaining food cards and German marks. He pressed them on the orderly, tearfully embracing him. "It's only thanks to you," he said, "that we've come out of this slaughterhouse in one piece!"

"One day you must write all that we've seen," Chamoin said.

"Write?" Céline's tone was that of a man naming something foreign to him. "To be read by whom? Tomorrow's conquerors? The Mongol hordes?"

Céline and Chamoin exchanged farewells. Lucette sat down on their bags to rest. Within seconds, she'd dropped off to sleep. Céline lay awake at her side. An hour went by. Had Chamoin's train left? Dizzy but vigilant, Céline tried to block out the explosive trebles of the orchestral locomotives in his head. He tried to concentrate on the further ordeals that awaited them. Complicated anxieties whirled through his mind until he could no longer keep track. A faraway look came over his face. "All this is very sad," he said out loud to no one.

"Oh yes!" A man in a German army uniform was standing a few feet away. "There's nothing else you can say about it."

Surprised, Céline glanced up at the soldier, a sandy-haired fellow in his thirties. He was immediately struck by the man's immobile, wide-open eyes, whose pupils seemed to dilate and contract without blinking as he looked at you. The doctor in Céline sensed something missing. He stared.

"Don't be troubled by my eyes," the soldier said. "The lids are gone, you see. Frozen off, one night in Smolensk. In deep cold, you don't notice variations of temperature. But you start to lose body parts. The same night I lost my eyelids, I also lost my hands." He raised his arms, showing Céline the bandaged stumps, then smiled and shook his head as if to wave off any expression of sympathy.

"I was lucky. I've still got my feet, and . . ." he bent forward, nodding toward his uniform belt, "and my balls. Out there, you know, a lot of guys lost theirs in the frost!"

"Where I'm coming from, a lot of guys lost theirs also, but not in frost," said Céline. "That's what you people have over us. Though, of course, we'll all lose everything in the end!"

"*Sicher,*" the soldier said, staring off into the smoky shadows of the station. Without lids, his pupils seemed to be the size of large blue cherries.

"I, too, am doomed to sleep with my eyes open," said Céline.

Shortly before dawn a train steamed into the station. It was made up of passenger carriages, but all the seats were taken. Riders were crowding the vestibules and clinging to the roof. Each carriage bore a huge Red Cross flag on its side. The train was carrying a sizable contingent of Swedish women and children out of German territory.

A Swedish Red Cross colonel stepped off onto the platform. Using the last of his strength, Céline assailed the colonel with arguments, pleas and cajoling. He begged to be taken to Denmark. But the colonel could not be persuaded. There was no room on the train. Refugees were storming the carriages, trying to shove themselves aboard. Soldiers pulled them off. Someone fired a shot into the air. In the middle of this chaos, the usually reticent Lucette intervened, stepping forth to spill out a surprising torrent of words. The colonel listened, nodded, finally smiled. Lucette rushed to Céline, hauled him and their last belongings on board.

Minutes later the train was moving slowly through the station, then flowing along over pristine track and roadbed as smoothly as a bullet going down the barrel of a rifle. Céline drifted into light, fitful sleep that opened out at the bottom into a dark tumble toward oblivion.

3.
COPENHAGEN

When Céline opened his eyes a cold light flooded in: the wakefulness of morning in a new world. As painful as it was abrupt, the light came too soon for the exhausted voyager. Having passed through hell, it would have been poetic justice for him to have awakened in heaven. But that was not how things worked out. You could fall through the bottom of chaos, but you were still lost: This was his first thought upon opening his eyes to the daylight of Copenhagen.

The railway station was unexpectedly calm. The crowds of refugees the travelers had encountered throughout Germany were nowhere to be seen. Céline and Lucette were soon standing on the street, under a white Danish sky that didn't much resemble heaven's; but at least it contained no spiraling flares, no shooting stars, no plumes of smoke or flame.

They felt lightheaded. Neither had eaten in twenty-four hours. Dragging their bags, they stumbled into a small grocery shop. Lucette, wide-eyed, cried out at the sight of so much food, her voice as high and ecstatic as an excited child's. Peals of giddy laughter tumbled out of her.

Céline grasped her arm and turned to the shopkeeper. "My wife's not well," he said in English. "Can you let us have some bread?" He fumbled in his pockets for some coins.

Moments later they were back in the street, chomping hungrily at big hunks of the dark bread they'd purchased. Céline, who remembered the city from previous visits, guided Lucette to a plaza towered over by a tall white building—the Hotel d'Angleterre. Their filthy, soot-blackened clothing and tattered baggage drew curious glances from the Danes who bicycled past them.

Inside the lobby of the hotel, a uniformed doorman intercepted them and blocked their way to the reception desk.

"I'm afraid we're all booked up."

Céline began to protest in English, but the doorman, who was twice as stout, continued to stand in his way.

"This is intolerable!" Céline's voice boomed through the baroque-style lobby. "Is this how you treat a regular client of your hotel?"

The clerk glanced around nervously. German officers were passing by on their way in and out of the hotel; several of them slowed down, measuring the spectacle with quizzical stares.

"Perhaps," the clerk said to Céline, "you'd care to see the manager?"

Céline nodded. The clerk bustled off, looking relieved. Moments later a tall, bespectacled man in a gray three-piece suit presented himself, announcing stiffly that he was the manager. With undisguised skepticism, he inquired whether the gentleman had really been a customer of the hotel.

"I've stayed here many times. Dr. Ferdinand Destouches, of the League of Nations."

Bowing with exaggerated politeness, the manager slipped around to the other side of the front desk and began leafing through some leatherbound registers. When he came back, he wore a thin smile.

"I'm sorry, doctor. Everything's in order. But you must forgive us. This is now the official residence of the German general staff. General Kaupnitz has ordered us to be very careful about who comes and goes. Certainly there's a room for you. But only for two or three nights, I'm afraid. . . . The general prefers that the rooms remain open, in case they're needed as quarters for officers on leave from the north."

Céline looked with dismay at Lucette.

"It's better than nothing," she said, managing a weary smile.

In fact there were plenty of rooms for them to choose from. The past eighteen months of German-imposed curfews and reprisals had given Copenhagen a taste of the reign of terror endured by other European capitals; as a result the hotel's civilian clientele had dwindled to a trickle. The German officers who'd requisitioned the first two floors could be seen strolling the lobby and terraces like uneasy impresarios of a failing production. They paraded up and down the broad canopied sidewalks along the Kongens Nytorv marketplace, discussing the latest war news in low voices. The café tables that lined the walks were bare, as the hotel management continued to observe the "shortened season" necessitated by the Occupation.

Céline and Lucette were given a room overlooking the old city and the theatrical little port, with its blue harbor and docked ships like toy boats in a bathtub.

They gave little notice to the view, falling stupefied into the spacious bed. Lucette slipped immediately into a profound sleep. But Céline's nerves were vibrating. He found it almost impossible to close his eyes. When at last he did, images of smoke and flames and burning bodies exploded under his lids: lingering, phosphenelike imprints of the horrors he'd passed through.

He got out of bed. While Lucette slumbered, he drew a curtain back and kept a silent vigil at the windows. Deep in the night there was an alert. The dark sky filled up with the bold, stabbing verticals and diagonals of searchlight beams, crisscrossing like the lances of the soldiers in Uccello's painting of battle. Céline braced himself for the shock to follow. But it didn't come. No hum of planes, no waterfall of flares, no explosions. "A mere drill," he said out loud to himself.

"They're only seeing to it that we don't get out of practice!" Lucette, accustomed to responding to his voice, stirred in her sleep. "It's nothing," Céline soothed her. "Only a fantasia, Luci! A ballet of lights for the voyagers!"

Around three in the morning, trucks with muffled head-lights rumbled slowly over the cobblestones below the window, followed by a string of dark forms on bicycles. Céline heard German being spoken. The voices sounded tense, clipped. The Germans were headed for the port, indicating the retreat from the north was already under way. Troops from Finland were being pulled back to the Fatherland. Gunmetal glinted in the weak moonlight. Céline stepped away from the window.

He slept lightly for an hour or two, then awoke in a cold sweat. He tried to go back to sleep, but the deep silence of the room only made him grow more and more restless. The silence accentuated the noises in his head—and his fears for the future.

Such anxieties weren't new to him, only more intense. His compulsive drive to put himself in dangerous situations had always stopped short of total financial disinterestedness. But that was something that went back to his childhood: the years of watching his mother and father treat every sou with the precautionary concern of a shepherd for the last sheep in the flock. They'd bred into him a sense of thrift that had survived even the most extreme of his self-sacrificial impulses.

In 1938, worried about the unstable political situation, he'd gone to Copenhagen and stored a cache of gold in a bank safe-deposit box there. During the Nazi Occupation of Paris, he'd maintained a policy of disdain and distance toward the city's conquerors. He'd compromised this policy on only one occasion, in 1942, when fears of the loss of his gold had forced him to make a trip to Berlin. The Germans had been confiscating bank accounts all over Europe, including one of his own in Amsterdam. Aware that his nest egg in Copenhagen was ripe for seizure, and unable to get there to withdraw it himself, he had done the next best thing. He'd asked Karen Jensen, an ex-girl friend who was touring Germany with the Danish National Ballet, to meet him in Berlin, and then —on the pretext of attending a medical conference in that city—had requested permission of the Germans to travel there.

He had put in only a brief pro forma appearance at the conference. When his German hosts had politely but firmly insisted he make himself useful by addressing a gathering at the French Workers' Institute, he'd instigated an uproar at the institute by telling the workers that the choice of allegiances between Germany and Russia was "a matter of choosing between cholera and the plague." Reports on this provocative speech had got back to S.S. headquarters. For the next few days Céline had noticed he was being followed wherever he went. Playing out the cloak-and-dagger role he'd created for himself, he'd set out from his hotel for a "walk" through crowded side streets, during which he'd managed to shake his plainclothes escort long enough to meet Karen Jensen in a café.

He'd given Karen the key to his Danish safe-deposit box, instructing her to withdraw the gold and hide it for him. She'd tried to persuade him to escape to Denmark and had offered him her apartment there. "They're watching me too closely now," he'd replied. "Besides, there's Lucette to worry about. One has to prepare one's departures."

During the remaining war years, news about the fate of his gold had come to him in coded letters from Karen, who'd written of "the children": "The children are safe . . . you need have no fears about the children." With the help of a cousin, Hella Johansen, Karen had withdrawn the gold from the bank; later, when Karen went away on tour, Hella had buried it—packed in a large metal biscuit box—in the back-yard of her family's country house south of Copenhagen. While Karen remained abroad, living in Madrid, the gold stayed in Hella Johansen's care. Now Céline had to find this woman he'd never met, and reclaim it.

Even worse, to discourage black marketeers, Denmark had instituted laws preventing private citizens from holding or trading in precious metals. If Céline did get his gold back, keeping it in his possession would be a crime. And then again . . .

Staring up through the dark at the hotel ceiling, he looked into a future whose shifting images mingled and separated moment by moment—playing across his consciousness like searchlight beams tracking a plane across a black sky. Finally a half-waking nightmare of being accused by disembodied voices and hunted down by faceless pursuers overtook him. He woke at dawn, unrefreshed and apprehensive.

.   .   .

Day broke clear and cold over the city. The rising sun flared up in a thousand reflected blazes on the city's decorative roofs and steeples, the three-hundred-year-old handiwork of the craftsmen of King Christian IV. Céline's daylight view of the city confirmed what he'd been told. Copenhagen had so far made it through the war undamaged, in its architecture if not in its spirit. The copper sheeting of the roofs threw back glints of green, blue and gold, a shimmering, multifaceted explosion of light.

Under the window bicyclists began to appear on the cobblestone streets around Kongens Nytorv square. The riders' bodies were huddled close to the handlebars for protection from a cold wind that Céline, secure in the hotel room, couldn't feel. The sun moved higher in the sky, casting warmer tones onto the stones of the apricot-colored buildings. The buildings slowly took on a borrowed radiance, as if light reflected from the copper roofs were being stored in them.

There was nothing radiant, however, in the human presence arrayed beneath Céline's eyes. A party of German soldiers loitered on a corner, evidently waiting for something. With their backs turned to the wind and shoulders hunched forward, their postures suggested extreme dejection. Perhaps it was only that they were freezing. One soldier bent with cupped hands to light a cigarette. Another uniformed man, this one in an officer's leather coat, said something to him. The soldier threw his cigarette to the pavement, where it landed in a shower of sparks swiftly carried off by the wind.

As he looked down at the unhappy poses of those soldiers, it struck Céline that their body language told a story the newspapers and radio dispatches hadn't yet reported: There was no more time left. The war was really over. This war, which had been nothing but a prolonged murder! With the civilized world as its victim! Now that the victim was dead, it was time for the postmortems to begin. The autopsy, the inquests . . . and, of course, the prosecutions of the accused.

That afternoon Céline and Lucette took a taxi to Hella Johansen's residence, a comfortable apartment in a good part of the city. Madame Johansen, a broad-shouldered blonde with her hair in a bun, greeted them amiably. She served them tea and pastries. Her attempts at small talk evoked only impatience in Céline, who quickly worked the conversation around to the gold. Hella assured him that it was safe. Céline, who'd frequently compared his own skeptical nature with that of St. Thomas, the Doubter, insisted on seeing for himself.

They went by car along the Sound to the Johansen country house. The hour's drive south along the seacoast gave Céline his first unhurried look at the country outside the capital. The German presence, so noticeable in Copenhagen, was much less apparent beyond the city limits. As they passed the big Italian-style castle on a hill at Frederiksberg, a convoy of armored vehicles rolled by, going the other way. After that there were few traces of the Nazi occupying forces. In this timeless landscape of forests, pastures and small farms, smoke spiraled from thatched cottages and big champagne-colored plowhorses with creamy-beige manes and tails labored across the early spring fields, followed by seagulls that swooped to capture worms turned up by the plows. Here and there a red cow that had managed to escape slaughter by the Germans grazed in a meadow demarcated by hedgerows and windbreaks. Property dividing lines were neatly defined by rows of larch and willow. Here was the opposite of the chaos of Germany—a well-thought-out, hand-tended pastoral civilization that looked as if it probably hadn't changed much in centuries.

"Almost makes you forget there's a war going on," Céline commented after a while.

"Now, yes," Hella Johansen said. She drove on in thoughtful silence for a few moments before speaking again. "A few months ago it was much easier to remember. Look over there." She gestured toward a stand of trees beside the road. The woods were already filling out with blooming primroses and hyacinths under the still-leafless beech trees. "Last fall," Hella said, "during the general strike, they blocked the road off at that spot with tanks. You couldn't get in or out of the city without permission from the *Wehrmacht*. There was sabotage. Somebody would blow up a warehouse or a dock, then they'd call in a lot of people for questioning. If they called you in for questioning, you were lucky if you weren't shot or sent off to a camp." She paused, looking straight ahead through the windshield to where an inlet made an indentation in the Sound which ran parallel with the highway. Ahead, the road curved around a small bay where the water surged shoreward in heavy gray-blue planes, cresting in small frilly whitecaps that folded over the rocky shore. "People were being shot every day. So if it looks peaceful, keep in mind there are many things in the past that people can't forget."

Céline's reply was not in his customary bantering tone. "There's no forgetting," he said with lowered voice.

At the Johansen estate, they dug up the metal biscuit box. Céline unwrapped and counted the gold pieces that had been tucked away safely inside it. After studying them for a moment, he put them back and asked Hella to re-bury the box until he'd made arrangements to exchange the gold for Danish currency.

Hella gave Céline the key to Karen Jensen's empty apartment at Twenty Ved Stranden, Copenhagen. He and Lucette moved in there. The flat was on the top floor of a large four-story structure, built in the classical style with ornamental facade and impressive views from its upper stories. To the rear, Karen's apartment looked out on a landscaped garden; in front, on a canal, and beyond that to the glittering green-gold roofs and towers of the city: the belfry of the Christiansborg Palace, the campanile of the Bourse—with its encircling stone dragons' tails—and the steeple of the Church of the Savior. Hella told Céline that Hans Christian Andersen had once occupied the building, a coincidence that intrigued him; Andersen, too, had been a great admirer of dancers.

In his flight from Paris, Céline had left behind a comfortable apartment of his own, full of books, paintings, furniture, as well as manuscripts of works in progress. He had no idea what had become of any of it; he assumed everything had been pillaged or destroyed. "Liberated," that was the current term for it! And where did he stand with the law? That was something else he had no way of knowing. He risked a letter to his former secretary, requesting news from Paris, and instructing her to address him under a false name—"H. Courtial," a mad inventor-character from *Death on the Installment Plan*.

The secretary wrote back, informing him that a warrant had just been issued for his arrest, and, even worse, that his mother had died, alone in Paris, just before his departure from Sigmaringen.

Marguerite Céline Guillou Destouches: Since the death of his father a few years earlier, she'd been his sole remaining link with a childhood he'd transposed in his novels into a period of black comedy, but which in reality had been an uninterrupted stretch of toil, his training ground in the endless drudgery of petit-bourgeois existence. All that remained to him of those times were a few distant memories of isolated sensations: gaslights, the steam of noodles cooking and the pain of sore feet from grueling hikes across Paris at his mother's side, visiting aristocratic homes to repair the lacework of "fine ladies." A life of duty and humiliation! Her qualities of self-denial and discipline had reemerged in his own nature. Without them how could he have risen out of the class of his birth, made it through medical school, become a writer? Now this tenacious woman, whose years of lacemaking had cost her her eyesight, had finally been released from her labors by death. She'd been buried in an unmarked grave, because her son had made her name infamous.

He'd never made up to her the "disgrace" inflicted by his books. As a doctor in Paris, he'd been able to turn up part-time work for her, selling patent medicines, but that small economic recompense had not deflected the humiliation she had experienced when politically motivated reviewers of *Death on the Installment Plan* had called him a "masturbation addict" and a "pornographer." To a "good woman" of her class, any deprivation of poverty would have been preferable to that. And her beloved Ferdinand had hardly been penitent; he'd boldly invited his critics, who'd written that he should be done away with, to come and get him!

"I was always too hard on her," he told Lucette. "It's a trait I got from her; she was always too hard on herself."

For days he wandered around the Copenhagen apartment in a stupor of remorse and grief.

Céline presented himself at military headquarters to have his German passport renewed. The officer on duty, a young fellow with tired eyes that suggested experience beyond his years, stamped the document grimly, then looked Céline over. "That'll that care of you for another year, doctor," he said. "But between you and me, before very long this passport will be something you'll want to be careful about showing."

· · ·

Through late April and into May, Céline kept watch at the windows. What he saw nourished his premonitory sense. The war was indeed approaching its close.

White Red Cross buses began to appear in the streets. The buses were jammed with men in gray prison clothes. Lucette, joining her husband at the windows, expressed curiosity. Who did he suppose was in those buses?

"Repatriated Danes from the camps, I bet," Céline said. "The Boches must've unlocked the gates."

One night they were listening to a BBC broadcast on Karen Jensen's radio when an announcer interrupted to report a news flash. The Germans had capitulated in Denmark. The announcer's tone was exultant. Céline and Lucette exchanged silent glances. Céline switched the radio off.

There was no blocking out the meaning of this news, however. Within hours, singing and yelling wafted up from the pavement under the windows. The next morning the street below was full of people—talking, waving, hugging, shaking hands. The celebrating went on all day and night. On the following day the dancers and beer drinkers had been replaced by truckloads of Resistance workers, who'd emerged from hiding and were directing traffic, stopping cars to interrogate the passengers.

Immured in the apartment, Céline had no way of finding out what was going on in the city beyond what he could see from his windows, and what little the BBC revealed. But that night, after a trip to the baker's, Lucette burst into the apartment breathless with rumors and reports. The English-speaking baker had told her the news: The Resistance had taken over Copenhagen and had already begun to purge the city of collaborators.

The wheels of judgment had begun to turn. In France, the purge of collaborators had already been going on for six months. Many writers had come to trial. Brasillach had been shot; Lucien Rebatet was in prison. Everyone who'd performed for the Germans was being arrested. If Céline himself hadn't been a performer, he'd known most of them.

He bought French newspapers and spent hours studying them, then discussing with Lucette the fates of people they'd known and comparing the cases to his own.

"I see where they've picked up Alfred Cortot," he said one day.

"The pianist?"

"Yes."

"What have they got on him?"

"He played piano for German radio." Céline laughed ironically. "The Courts of Justice are far more interested in bumping off clowns and jugglers than in catching up with the real *collabos*. Look at the brokers of the black market. Or the guys who took contracts to build the Atlantic wall. They're all thriving! The ones who made millions off the war, who played the stock exchange of history like touts at Longchamps, rubbed knees with Gestapo tarts in nightclubs, and bought themselves chateaux and diamonds and furs and gold; oh, they were clever, all right! Joined up with the Resistance at the last possible minute! And now they're free as birds! Naturally!

No, the courts would prefer to have the skin of some piano player or dancer, while the real villains in this farce lounge on the Midi!"

Lucette nodded. "My mother writes that Nice and Menton are full of Vichy civil servants."

Céline continued to scan the newspaper in his lap. "Remember that actress, Jeanette, the one who used to hang around with the guy from Abetz's staff? We met her at Moll Peters' once?"

"The big one with red hair?"

"She's been arrested, too, for associating with the enemy."

"For sleeping with that German?"

"Yes. She's reported as having said, 'Regardless of what my sex was doing, my heart was always French!' "

Lucette fidgeted, the small muscles in her neck involuntarily tensing.

Céline set the paper down. "We'll just have to remain invisible a while longer."

She stared at him. "How long?"

"Until they've forgotten I exist."

Then came events that would make forgetfulness impossible.

Céline wanted to bathe in the rivers that flow beyond memory, those streams of forgiveness that after most wars spring up from the dry rocks of suffering and gradually wash away men's crimes, leaving the heroes secure with their medals and stories, the villains mercifully forgotten in the daily routine of life to be lived.

But then, spreading out his precious French newspapers one day, he saw bold headlines trumpeting fresh revelations of horror. Beneath these shocking banners unfolded the first-hand accounts of concentration-camp survivors. The stories in the daily journals soon turned into serials, the serials into full-scale magazine features, detailing cruelties unparalleled in history.

More ominous still were the photos taken by Allied armies as they entered the camps—gruesome images that made the worst nightmares seem benign in comparison. *Here,* then, was the work of the Aryan conquerors—those final defenders of the white race! Céline sat over the papers for hours, sickened, unable to speak even to Lucette when she tried to console him by reminding him that he *hadn't known.* . . .

That was no consolation, he saw. He had set himself up as a seer. And what else is demanded of the seer, but to *know*?

As the uncovered truths from the camps sank in, the blunt, bruising numbness of disbelief turned slowly to cold fear like an icepick in his heart. He'd been careful never to collaborate with the Nazis, yes—but that wasn't going to save him now! For his prewar pamphlets still existed, an unanswerable indictment in hundreds of thousands of copies. Their very titles echoed as menacing evidence, an oracular language of apocalypse: *Bagatelles pour un massacre, L'École des cadavres.* . . . That he had neither foreseen nor taken part in the Nazis' insane crimes against the species wouldn't excuse him: The pamphlets would be taken as incitements, a criminal goading of the genocidal beast.

Looking down at the photos from the camps, his mind's

eye stared through them, making out the shadows of words he'd written a decade earlier—in that time, which now felt like another century, when everything had seemed so intelligible to him. His own motives most of all! Hadn't he wanted, above everything, simply to warn his fellow Frenchmen of the mortal dangers of war? Dangers that he, as a victim of the First War, understood all too well? He'd spoken in the wailing voice of Cassandra, as a wild-eyed, half-crazy herald of doom, announcing over and over that the Jews were pushing Europe toward a catastrophic war that would be the ultimate expression of their eternal profit motive. Remembering his words now, he shuddered, hearing behind them the raging tirades of his father, holding forth against Dreyfus over plates of noodles at the family dinner table on the Passage Choiseul.

His father had considered himself a personal victim of persecution at the hands of Jews. Céline remembered that too well. And his own similar feelings. How he'd been badly used by his Jewish boss at the League of Nations, and then later by the Russian Jew—in fact a Communist spy, hadn't he known it all along—at the municipal clinic of Clichy, where he'd been driven out by the Russo-Semitic conspiracy! Thinking back to these experiences made the blood rise to his head all over again, bringing on the sensations of hatred that had inspired him to write his polemics. A tidal flood of blood and feeling! Experiences that were too numerous and consistent to dismiss as coincidences . . . the Hollywood lawyer who'd stolen from him the first dancer he'd loved, Elizabeth Craig, not only stolen her but corrupted her with

Semitic evils, with money and drugs . . . Hollywood, the source of the lie that was the modern world . . . he'd been there, he'd seen it, he knew! As he'd been to Moscow, Hollywood's twin sister in the repressive deception of men! Oh, he'd seen it, he'd been speaking from experience . . . and yet . . . and yet . . . these pictures from the camps . . .

His mind whirled, a turbulent sea of anger, confusion, remorse and apprehension . . . one thing, and only one thing, was clear: For him, the war was far from over. The world's agony was drawing him to its center. The time of healing he'd anticipated didn't exist. In its place had come only a fearful time of remission.

Who could say how long that time was going to last? As long as it lingered on, one had to try to consider the future and to take practical measures for living through the period of waiting.

The high cost of living in Copenhagen had come as a surprise to Céline. The food-ration cards he received from Hella Johansen weren't enough to feed two people. And although he paid her for the cards, the arrangement troubled him, because it put him further in Hella's debt. His personal policy had always been to owe nothing to anybody. He had grave qualms about accepting favors, and accepting them from someone who was a virtual stranger made him even more uneasy.

The only way he could qualify for ration tickets of his own was to register with the Danish police. But he hesitated to go to the police alone. Who knew what might happen? He needed a lawyer. A neighborhood pharmacist supplied him with a reference: Thorvald Mikkelsen. Mikkelsen had worked for the Danish Resistance, the pharmacist said. When the look on Céline's face told him he'd said the wrong thing, the pharmacist quickly added that Mikkelsen was also known to be a great admirer of the French; a widower, he'd been long and happily married to a Frenchwoman, whose memory he now revered. Mikkelsen read French literature and vacationed in Paris every winter, the pharmacist said.

Céline went to the lawyer's office. Mikkelsen was a small, stout fellow with thinning silver hair, a bluff manner and a habit of squinting nearsightedly through his glasses as he talked. It was true, he spoke excellent French and had even read *Journey to the End of the Night* and *Death on the Installment Plan*. He greeted Céline warmly—and, after inquiring into his circumstances, agreed to help him.

A few days later Mikkelsen went to the head of the Danish national police, announced Céline's presence and requested a residence permit on his behalf. Considering his client's precarious state of health, refusing him the permit might amount to endangering his life, the lawyer suggested.

The police summoned Céline for an interview. Overcoming his trepidation—after all, he had no choice in the matter— he went. Mikkelsen, who accompanied him, advised him to disclose everything. Accordingly Céline told his story as best he could, including his injuries in the First War, his life as a doctor and a writer—even mentioning his anti-Semitic pamphlets—and said he'd come to Denmark to live off savings he'd put in the keeping of Danish friends before the war.

The interview went off without a hitch. The police treated Céline courteously, and when it was over they issued residence permits allowing him and Lucette to dwell legally in Copenhagen and to obtain food rations. The couple was ordered to report every week to a special police office in the city, where ration cards would be supplied.

Mikkelsen, however, cautioned them that as foreigners they would not be permitted to work. "But don't worry about that," he told them. "I'll take care of it in time."

Late in June the lawyer invited Céline and Lucette to a party at his Copenhagen home. Among those present were the Danish minister of special affairs, some former members of the national Resistance and several doctors from the city's main hospital. Mikkelsen had planned the party solely to get Céline an invitation to practice in the national hospital. But the impression the guest of honor made at the party was not at all what Mikkelsen had hoped for. Céline's efforts at sociability were belied by the anxiety engraved on his face, and by the hard edge of cynicism that created a hollow ring in his attempts to make small talk. Even worse, when politics came up, he forgot his good intentions and made remarks he regretted as soon as they'd slipped from his mouth. Those in earshot exchanged uneasy glances. Mikkelsen may have described the visitor as an innocuous medical man, but the fellow's conversation was something else again. For instance, he actually seemed to believe the Russians would soon conquer Europe, with the Chinese not far behind! The hospital's chief of staff took Mikkelsen aside and politely explained that there were no places open at the hospital.

If the medical men at the party were cool toward Céline, the Resistance veterans were downright hostile. Céline had been careful to have Mikkelsen introduce him as "Dr. Destouches" and to conceal the fact that he was a writer. But having been in Germany was black mark enough, it appeared. Most of the lawyer's Resistance friends seemed to know he'd been there, and certain comments of Céline's—he referred in passing, for instance, to the devastation of the bombed cities—made it evident to the rest.

After the party Céline vowed to Lucette he'd never again go out in public in Copenhagen. "Just think of it—copies of the *Journey* in Danish lying around Mik's house! It's not worth the risk! And besides, did you see the looks I got? They'd no sooner have me working in their national hospital than perform brain surgery on a baboon there!"

Unable to practice medicine for a living, Céline had no choice but to live off his limited reservoir of gold. Receiving it in small increments from Hella Johansen, he exchanged it through certain Copenhagen jewelers who did business "on the quiet." But what with the inflated cost of shopping on the black market—food was short, and rations were always inadequate—the money seemed to disappear as fast as Céline could get his hands on it.

To make ends meet, Lucette decided to take on students. But lacking a work permit, she'd have to teach under an assumed name. Through a ballet professor to whom she'd been referred by Karen Jensen, she obtained the use of a studio, but the professor demanded a large share of what she earned. Borrowing shoes, tights, a dress and a set of castanets from Karen Jensen's wardrobe, she began instructing young Danish girls in Spanish dance. She was happy to be working again. After a few weeks, however, the share of her earnings demanded by the professor started going up. To compensate, she took on another class, which met in the back room of a fish shop near Copenhagen's central fish market. Because this one was a class in Oriental dance, she had to buy costumes; to pay for them, she had to take on more pupils. Before long she was teaching every day of the week, even on Sundays, when she snuck into a rehearsal studio at the Copenhagen Opera to coach some young dancers from the national company.

Lucette's stamina was now the couple's best resource. The physical exertion of her classes was only a prelude to shopping expeditions that required hours of wrestling through long ration lines, but even after such marathon days, coming back to the apartment with her armful of packages, she was always able to manage a smile for her husband and to prepare the dinners that gave them both the strength to continue—and through which they sat in silence.

The long days in the apartment had come to weigh heavily on Céline. Time, he was beginning to find, has a special weight for someone in exile. He felt himself adrift, like a sailor whose becalmed boat floats in aimless circles. For the first time in his adult life, he wasn't working. That, perhaps, was the worst torment of the present phase of his exile.

For as long as he could remember, work had been his life. He'd once been famous for that—it was a standing joke with his friends. Working on his novels, he'd barely taken time out to eat. Coming in from the clinic in those days, he'd slip a slice of cold ham into his pocket, go to his desk and nibble at the ham as he began writing himself into a trance that might not end until the next morning. And this had been his routine seven days a week; on Sunday mornings he'd drop in at his friend Gen Paul's weekly social gatherings, but only long enough to taste the conversation, feed his appetite for the rhythms of speech, store up material for the writing that occupied him so completely. One day he'd varied this routine long enough to act on a decision involving his latest paramour, the young dancer Lucette Almanzor. "Let's get married," he'd suddenly suggested; before she could do more than nod in agreement he'd jumped on his motorcycle, headed for the notary's office. Lucette had followed behind on her bicycle through Paris traffic, too shocked to do anything but obey the will of this strange fellow who resembled no other man she'd met. Later that same day he'd been back at his desk again, churning out more pages to attach by clothespins to the strings that crisscrossed his Montmartre apartment like trolley wires.

Back then there had never been enough time to satisfy him. Now, though, with time on his hands and visions of chaos still simmering in his head, he found that his imagination had gone cold on him. Ever since the voyage through Germany, he'd experienced a deepening sense of fatigue and lassitude. Throbbing migraines came on in waves, leaving him in an enervated stupor.

On summer days the heat of the sun on the roof tile made the apartment uncomfortably warm. Céline relieved himself of clothing, exposing the flesh that comprised his one remaining claim to membership in humanity. It seemed to hang slack, independent of the soul it had once inhabited—this body that had carried him through so much to arrive here and still survived to bear whatever punishments men might devise for him.

Naked at his desk, he spent long periods communing in silence with Bébert. The old cat sat placidly before him, atop a pile of blank manuscript pages. Looking into those unblinking, impartial feline eyes, Céline sometimes felt as though he were gazing into a mirror. The reflection of an ancient neutrality, something prior to the motives and feelings of persons, flickered back at him with a copper-amber hardness, aloof and almost serene in its inhuman severity—like the empty eyes of statues of pharaohs, or the cratered surfaces of dead worlds on the other side of the sun. In the end it overpowered him, making him look away. "Even Bébert thinks I'm no longer alive," he said to himself.

From the ballet professor Lucette heard rumors about shootings of Danish collaborators. These assassinations, it was being said, were only the beginning of a final purge that would remove from Denmark—and from existence—all those individuals suspected of colluding with the Nazis.

"The nets are closing," Céline told his wife in a somber voice that suggested more than it said. He began to develop an intense fear of being recognized. Like an animal that blends into its surroundings to avoid being attacked, he tried to become as inconspicuous as possible, seldom risking public exposure. Social life of any kind was now out of the question. In the mornings, if the weather was good, he still walked in the garden with Bébert; and once a day, acting out of a need for his native language that was even stronger than his fear of death, he cautiously ventured as far as a nearby newsstand that carried French papers. For form's sake it was necessary to exchange a word or two with the news dealer. The man spoke a little French. They chatted about the weather or about the headlines in the papers. Two or three perfunctory sentences in French, that was all. And of course there was risk even in that.

Spending long days alone in the apartment, he felt himself losing touch with the real world, and especially with its temporal orders. His mind slipped loose of its moorings in the present and cruised in wide arcs across the past, like one of those Breton trawlers he'd loved to watch on his holidays at Saint-Malo. The beings he fished up in those reveries were watery ghosts; contact with them increased his own sense of insubstantiality. Writing to Karen Jensen in Madrid, he mentioned to her in an ironic way that he was very busy. Every day, he said, he had to make the rounds of his own heart many times. Living among her possessions, he told her, he often ran into her there.

At the end of summer, Mikkelsen told Céline that there was someone he wanted him to meet: the Copenhagen chief of police. Céline demurred; the very word "police" made him nervous. But Mikkelsen insisted.

He invited Céline and Lucette to dinner with the police chief and his family. The chief was a large, fair-haired man whose good manners and proper English reminded Céline of the bankers he'd dealt with at Lloyd's in London; he treated Céline quite civilly, as a distinguished visitor who happened to be in difficult circumstances. No mention was made of the fact that in France there was now an arrest warrant on Céline's head. Céline wondered: Did this mean the warrant remained unknown to Danish authorities? *Could* it be they didn't know?

The chief's only allusion to Céline's precarious legal status came near the end of the evening, when Mikkelsen remarked that this had been his client's first social outing in months. "Our French friend has been like the invisible man," the lawyer said in his customary droll tone. He winked conspiratorially at the police chief. "We must see to it that he gets out more, don't you think? There's so much to see in our country, it's a crime to let such an intelligent man waste away alone in that stuffy apartment."

The chief's expression turned doubtful. He was silent for

a moment. "In the present climate," he said finally, obviously choosing his words with care, "it might be the wisest thing to go on exercising a certain amount of discretion in that regard."

One afternoon in the week following the dinner at Mikkelsen's, Céline left the apartment at his usual hour to traverse the few blocks to the newsstand. The early part of the day had been cool, misty, with the hint of an autumnal chill in the air. But now a fresh sea breeze had dispersed the thin morning fog, and the bicyclists who were gliding past in twos and threes wore only light sweaters. Céline, prepared for the worst as always, was bundled in a heavy wool overcoat, with a scarf pulled up around his head. The passing bicyclists regarded him with interest. He must be a foreigner; this early in the season, no Danish native would resort to an overcoat. Here was a fellow who looked as if he had something to hide.

It was not the weather but his fear of prying stares that made Céline tuck his head down into his scarf as he walked. Suppose the wrong person noticed him? He pulled himself along, punishing the sidewalk with his cane, keeping his eyes fixed on the end of the street dead ahead.

The open-air newsstand was located on a corner. Reaching it, he surveyed the day's headlines, wary of being under scrutiny whenever a car went past. You could never make yourself small enough. He shrank deeper into his scarf.

"This will interest you." The news dealer, a thin, wizened fellow in a cap, was pointing to *l'Humanité*.

"No, I'll take this one." Céline pulled a copy of *le Figaro* off its rack.

The dealer shrugged. "There's something in the other one."

"Oh?" Céline looked down at *l'Humanité*. The lead article was about war criminals on the run from the Courts of Justice. "NOWHERE TO HIDE!" proclaimed its subheadline. "I'll take this one, too," he said, folding both papers under his arm and handing the news dealer a coin. He felt the man's stare digging into his back as he turned to walk away, hurrying back to the apartment.

Mikkelsen, who owned an extensive library, had offered to lend Céline any books he wanted. He supplied a list of volumes, from which his client put in orders. To the lawyer's surprise, Céline ignored the modern authors on the list, borrowing only classic works from the nineteenth century and earlier. The exchange of volumes provided Mikkelsen with an opportunity to light up a pipe, prop his feet atop one of Karen Jensen's hassocks and bandy ideas with the famous author. Not that these sessions were always amicable. Mikkelsen's sanguine view of human nature and motives often butted head-on into Céline's own cynical outlook, summed up by the latter in the phrase, "Aim low, aim true."

On one such visit to Ved Stranden, Mikkelsen brought along a volume Céline hadn't requested. It was a selection from the works of Nietzsche, in a French translation.

Céline looked at the book's title page with distaste, then closed it and handed it back.

"Nietzsche! Haven't we just seen where that superman business leads? Nietzsche, up in his eyrie like some character out of Wagner! Forever talking about the lust of men to be more than themselves. 'Lust wants eternity,' that's what he says. But there's no eternity, Mik. Men die. Even Nietzsche. No, I've had enough of all that."

"Please. I've marked some passages I want you to read—where he talks about revenge."

Mikkelsen set the book down on a table and left it there.

A week later, one idle afternoon when Lucette was out, Céline picked up the volume and began leafing through the passages Mikkelsen had marked. They were from *Thus Spoke Zarathustra*—the second part, "On Deliverance."

Before long he was reading slowly and with care.

Revenge, Nietzsche was saying, is a mechanism of the human will. It expresses the revulsion of the will against the passing of time, which makes it suffer so. But revenge is always devious, Nietzsche went on to say. It never calls itself by its own name. Instead it calls itself "punishment," and covers itself over with a cloak of ethical propriety, pretending to be the instrument of historical justice-in-action.

"Exactly!" Céline muttered to himself.

"That man be delivered from revenge," Nietzsche concluded, *"that is for me the bridge to the highest hope."*

Céline took a pencil and began scrawling notes in the book's margin: "This deliverance can never happen. The human desire for vengeance is caught in time forever, like a fish in a net. Hope is for fools. There's no bridge left to cross!"

At the beginning of October 1945, an anonymous letter arrived at the French embassy in Copenhagen. The notorious collaborator L.-F. Céline was hiding out in the city, announced the letter writer. It was the first anybody at the embassy had heard of Céline's presence. Ambassador Guy de Charbonnière, a former civil servant who was new to diplomatic work, relayed the informer's tip directly to his superior, the French foreign minister in Paris. Wouldn't it be proper, Charbonnière asked, to request the Danish government to arrest this notorious collaborator and turn him over for extradition? He requested information on Céline and instructions on how to proceed with the case.

Ten days later the foreign minister replied, confirming that Céline was indeed wanted by the French Courts of Justice. The ambassador was instructed to notify Danish authorities and to ask them to take whatever measures they considered necessary. He was also supplied with a list of the French government's charges against Céline. Compiled hastily and without much research, the charges were sketchy; only the flimsiest evidence could be found against the accused, but this thin tissue had long since been reinforced by the hard steel of public opinion. In Resistance circles the name *Céline* had come to be synonymous with *evil*. The fact that the dossier on Céline sent out from Paris to Ambassador Charbonnière carried little legal weight didn't keep it from representing a heavy burden of historical judgment, written—as it were— between the lines.

Charbonnière forwarded a summary of the dossier to the Danish police, who took no immediate action on the case.

The days contracted. With the first bitter nights of winter came thick constellations of hoarfrost across the windows, draining the warmth out of the feeble yellow light of morning. A spume of whitish fog settled over the city, muffling the sound of boats in the harbor, the bicycles and seabirds below the windows; into the silence, snow fell, at first in thick white clusters like chunks of bread, then in thin driving particles. Sleet mixed with salt into a gray porridge on the streets.

The apartment was not adequately insulated. Céline, not yet recovered from the physical ordeal of his flight into exile, was very susceptible to cold. No matter how many wool sweaters and scarves he put on, nothing could keep his teeth from chattering as he sat at his work desk, writing nothing. He got up and walked around the apartment, talking to himself to keep his mind off the chill he felt.

One day he opened up his battered trunk, pulled out the unfinished manuscript of a novel and set to work at it. The old heat of creation was slow in coming. To pour out his sorrows in the language of the heart, that would be too painful to bear! He struggled to recover the tone of levity and burlesque he'd always employed in his books, to make them

bearable. But that tone was an element of his writing rep-
ertoire that depended to a large extent on his surroundings.
To transpose emotion, he'd always found, you had to use
the spoken language. Now, cut off from the stream of spoken
French that had formerly provided not only his environment
as a writer, but his best source of inspiration, he felt lost
when he looked down at the blank paper.

Fiddling with the radio dials one evening after Lucette had
gone off to bed, he happened across a static-blurred broadcast
of French popular music from Paris. A woman was singing
a *chanson* he'd heard thousands of times, in better days. As
familiar to him as the letters in his own name, the sentimental
song meant nothing to him, but the language in which it was
sung brought tears to his eyes. The fragmentary broadcast
was soon lost among the ions of the night.

On November 23 the French foreign minister wired Ambassador Charbonnière, directing him to request the extradition of Céline. Charbonnière conveyed the request to
Danish authorities. Still no action was taken by the Danes.

Céline himself had no idea that a dossier detailing his "crimes"
had been filed with Danish officials. And so of course he had
no idea what was happening to that dossier in the Copenhagen governmental bureaus through which it moved—nor
that, in fact, it had stopped moving at all. The Danish minister
of special affairs, unable to decide what to do about the ag-
onizing matter of the famous French writer whose head was
wanted by his countrymen, had managed to "lose" the dos-

sier by letting it fall from the top of a radiator into the crevice behind, where it remained unseen for several months.

One day in early December Céline got another letter from his former secretary in Paris. This one concerned Robert Denoël, his publisher. Denoël, to whose office he'd once ridden on his motorcycle with the manuscript of the *Journey* in a locked briefcase chained to his wrist! The same Denoël who'd in turn come looking for him a few weeks later, curious about the identity of this pseudonymous author who'd left a shocking masterpiece sitting on his editorial desk. That had been the beginning of this whole sad affair—not only for Céline but for Denoël himself.

Denoël had other authors, but for better or worse, it was Céline who'd made the publisher's reputation—with the great, controversial explosions of the novels, and equally with the grotesque fireworks of the polemical pamphlets that followed. Céline's books had a way of getting under people's skin like drops of some corrosive acid, and it was impossible to think of Denoël without thinking of them. If Céline's fame as a writer had rubbed off on the publisher, so had his infamy.

The news brought by the letter was this: Denoël had somehow survived the Liberation without leaving Paris. He'd holed up in his apartment for nearly a year and a half, emerging only when it was absolutely necessary. Finally, on the evening of the second day of December 1945, he'd decided it was safe to reappear in public. Accompanied by his mistress, who was also his business partner, he'd gone out in his car for an evening at the theater. En route, he'd had a flat tire on the Place des Invalides. He'd stopped to change the tire, but since he was without proper tools, his mistress had headed off on foot toward the nearest police station, allegedly in search of assistance. When the police arrived at the scene, they found Denoël on his face, with several bullets in his back. His wallet, full of money, was still with his body.

Céline reacted to this news as if he'd been shot along with his publisher. He sat back, limp in his chair, with the pages of the letter from Paris spilled across his lap—and hadn't moved from that position by the time Lucette came in from the ballet studio. He handed her the letter. As she read it, her face went white. She dropped into a chair at his side.

They sat in silence for a while. Slowly the color came back into Lucette's cheeks. "You know," she said tentatively, "murders happen every day." She glanced at her husband. "Maybe this had nothing to do with us?"

Céline shook his head, adamant. "No, it's perfectly clear."

"But why?"

"Either the Jews commissioned it, or the Resistance did. Either way, I was the ultimate target."

"You're forgetting the woman. She could have had her own reasons. She was there, wasn't she?"

Céline stared at his wife.

"With Denoël out of the picture," Lucette continued, "isn't the business in her hands?"

Céline thought for a moment. "Regardless of who killed Denoël, it's bad news for us." He stood up slowly, as if lifting a great weight, and went to the windows. Gulls were riding the strands of mist that drifted rapidly across the bluish metal rooftops. "A terrible wind is blowing, Luci! I can feel it." Looking out over the city, he shivered and pulled his large, loose sweater tighter around his body.

Mikkelsen sailed off on a three-month vacation to America. Before leaving, he assured Céline that there was nothing to worry about, legally speaking. The police chief was sympathetic; Céline was now a legal resident; everything was in order.

"Perhaps," Céline replied doubtfully. "Who knows what to believe?"

"Ever the skeptic!" Mikkelsen laughed. "If there's any problem, call my partner."

"And who shall I call if the Resistance shows up at my door to bump me off?"

"Call the police, of course!"

Céline eyed the lawyer suspiciously. "Your trip wouldn't happen to have anything to do with me, would it?"

On December 15, the Paris weekly *Samedi-Soir* published the first journalistic revelation of Céline's presence in Denmark. The tone of the article was not that of a news story, but of a sensational exposé. By Sunday the sixteenth, the item had been picked up by the Danish left-wing daily *Politiken*. Its front-page coverage went *Samedi-Soir* one better, portraying the French writer as a monster in Denmark's midst. His anti-

Semitic books, said *Politiken,* had understandably given rise
to the belief that Céline was insane. The article stated—erroneously—that he had fled with the Vichy government to
Sigmaringen and concluded with the suggestion that he was
now living comfortably in Denmark off prewar royalties
stashed in a Danish bank.

When Céline went to buy the papers that afternoon, his
conversation with the news dealer was as cursory as usual,
but he couldn't help feeling the man was sizing him up with
a new degree of interest. Though he didn't notice the stack
of copies of *Politiken* with his face on the front page, the
dealer's behavior bothered him all the way home. He resolved
to seek out another place to buy newspapers.

Even before Céline got back to the apartment, the news
dealer had closed his stand for the day and was on the telephone with a duty officer at the Danish government bureau
of investigation.

That evening Lucette had a surprise caller. It was the stepdaughter of the chief of police. This woman, who'd been
present during their dinner with the chief at Mikkelsen's, had
later sent her own daughter to Lucette for dance lessons. Since
then they'd maintained friendly relations, although Lucette
had only seen her two or three times.

The woman appeared flustered, as if she had something on
her mind. Lucette's attempts at small talk fell flat. Finally the
chief's stepdaughter blurted out that trouble was coming.
She took Lucette's hand and spoke in a breathless rush. "Get

out of the city! Out of Denmark, if you can! If you don't, you'll wind up in jail!"

Lucette confronted the woman: "What are you talking about? We're registered with the authorities!" She turned to her husband, who was across the room, sitting at his desk.

Céline stood up. "I'm sure you've made a mistake," he told the police chief's stepdaughter. "As you can see, we've been living here like mice. We've done nothing!"

"The whole thing's in the newspapers," the woman cried. She squeezed Lucette's wrist. "Go to Sweden with your husband before it's too late!"

Drifting in and out of restless sleep that night, Céline was suddenly brought to full alertness by a loud noise in the apartment. It sounded like heavy furniture being pushed around. His hair stood on end, and he felt cold drops of sweat on his forehead. Reaching for the loaded pistol he'd become accustomed to keeping on his bedside table, he got out of bed and began prowling the apartment. Brilliant moonlight flooding in the windows provided enough illumination to allow him to quickly establish that there was no intruder.

When he went back into the bedroom, the bedside light was on. Lucette was sitting bolt upright in bed, her face taut with fright.

"What is it? Those noises—is someone here?"

"It's nothing." He climbed back into bed.

"Are you sure?"

"I looked around."

"I thought someone was breaking chairs and tables. The whole flat was . . . I don't know—creaking!"

"I heard it too. It sounded like what those table tappers call 'raps'—some kind of message from the world beyond, perhaps a warning. *Merde!* We've had enough warnings for one day!"

Céline flicked the light switch, returning cold blue starlight to the room. Lucette went back to sleep, but he continued to lie awake, listening, until morning.

The following day—the seventeenth—Céline and Lucette doubled their usual precautions. They stayed away from the windows, kept both door locks bolted and didn't set foot outside the apartment. When nothing out of the ordinary had occurred by nightfall, they relaxed their vigilance at least to the extent of permitting Bébert to tour the garden, Lucette accompanying him. The night was once again cold, with the clarity of a million stars. Lucette stayed out only five minutes, aware that her husband would be worried about her.

After dining modestly as usual, on herring and black bread, they prepared for bed. At that moment the French ambassador, Charbonnière, was on the phone with the Danish minister of foreign affairs.

The first loud knock at the door was followed by a series of peremptory commands in Danish. Céline sat up and listened, certain that this time it wasn't spirits from another world.

He swung his legs to the floor, began tugging his trousers on under his nightshirt.

Lucette slipped into a robe, scrambled to the front of the apartment, picked up the telephone receiver, then slammed it back down. The knocking at the door grew louder. Céline rushed into the room and began flinging windows open. He beckoned in an urgent whisper to Lucette, but she'd gone back into the bedroom to get their pistol.

Céline clambered out onto the roof. Its steeply pitched metal surface was slick with ice. He tried to grapple his way up to the roof peak. Overhead, the starshine was like flakes of dry ice scattered on a sky of pure mica. The city lights gave off a cold greenish glow like that of stage lighting. Under the weight of the whole northern sky, Céline struggled for his freedom. He pushed forward on one knee, but lost his grip and started to slip. *Merde!* He had to flatten himself against the roof to keep from sliding all the way down. The street whirled below.

Lucette suddenly appeared at the open window, clutching the pistol, and started to climb out onto the roof.

"I can't do it," Céline cried down to her. Moving crablike on all fours, he inched his way back to the window, then dropped into the apartment. His disheveled hair and nightshirt were dusted with frost.

The banging at the door continued. Voices rang out in Danish, then in English: "Police!"

With a defeated gesture Céline released the door latch. Three Danish plainclothesmen burst inside. Lucette screamed. One of the plainclothesmen noticed the loaded pistol lying

on a table and made a move for it. Bébert, who'd been crouch-
ing on the table, sprang out of the way, landing across the
room in a furry explosion at the foot of a second policeman.
Through the open windows a gust of wind surged in, lifting
a sheaf of loose papers off Céline's desk. The papers swirled
in the air like seabirds in a storm.

The policemen moved quickly around the apartment, pulling things apart. One found an enema bag; another was walking around holding a handful of rubber nozzles and tubes; a
third had turned up a syringe. Out came the contents of
Céline's medical bag, scattered on the floor. There were vials
of chemicals, sachets, powders.

Céline frantically waved his residence papers. The officers
paid little attention. They conferred in Danish, evidently
speculating as to what they'd found.

Céline slumped into a chair and covered his face with trem-
bling hands.

4. PRISON

He lay on his back on a wooden board in the dark. . . .

So this was where it got you, all that tempting of fate.

Put a blindfolded man in a cave and ask him where he is. . . . Or in a barn, a well, a hangar, a bank vault, a cathedral . . . How does one fathom the shape of nothingness?

To the prisoner this hollow, echoing darkness felt like the hold of a sinking ship.

Once before he'd felt that, and then his intuition had been correct. That had been years ago: lying in his bunk, deep inside the armored merchant ship *Chella,* at the beginning of the last war. Off the Spanish coast . . . There again, sticking

your neck out—the French patriot—see where it got you!
Ship's doctor, when he could have stayed home in Montmartre, "unfit for service"! There'd been a groaning shudder
deep in the night, pitching him out of the bunk! Midway in
the Marseilles-Casablanca run, they'd collided with an English vessel steaming out of Gibraltar. The *Chella* was going
down! Fires amidship! Men were hurt, burned, drowning.
A great quaking deep inside the hold . . .

He lay on his back listening. Around him the vast old
prison, with its open corridors and tiers that carried cross
echoes and resonances as a constant unquiet cargo, sailed
noisily into the endless night.

No, not sinking . . . but bound nowhere all the same.
Which was worse, the bottom of the ocean or the end of the
night?

Sleep . . .

It wasn't possible. He forced his eyes shut, pressing on the
lids with his fists until he saw starbursts. Time passed . . .
or did it? Men in other parts of the jail yelled, called to each
other, sang, cried women's names, chittered like monkeys,
prayed, wept, hooted at God. Somewhere metal doors clanged.
A guard announced the hours in a voice that ricocheted from
tier to tier. *Kloken to! Kloken tre!*

Each hour seemed to have a malign purpose all its own,
like a mad composer bent on making his audience share each
progressive stage of his derangement.

From two to three, for example, that strange groaning
sound. Was it huge wooden oars creaking, or perhaps a giant
screw being turned on a rack big enough to hold a thousand

guilty men? Somewhere up there in the dark, the tension was getting greater and greater. No blocking it out! Even when he pushed his thumbs into his ears, the sound continued, mingling with the phantom noise in his head.

The minutes went by like slow boats carrying a crew of banshees across an ocean with no shores.

Vestre Faengsel: the Prison of the West. His first night they dragged him out of a police van and left him alone in a reception cell in the prison's entry block. In the morning a guard came. Summoning a combination of his best English and the few Danish words he could muster, Céline begged for news of his wife. The guard shook his head, unable to comprehend, and led him off to a new cell in one of the main blocks.

It was an interior block near the heart of the prison. Here, none of the cells had windows. An unpleasant stale odor hung on the air, reminding Céline of the foul air of the town morgue in Clichy. Though in this case the ambient stench of decomposition wasn't coming from the dead but from the living, the similarity was still too close for comfort. Céline sat on the cot they'd provided him, sniffing at the noxious atmosphere. No doubt the same quantity of air had been recirculating through the lungs of the poor bastards in this block for months—even years! Every time it passed through, it got a little more depleted. . . . So that by now anybody who took a breath wasn't sucking in any oxygen at all, only the accumulated waste of a hundred other respiratory systems. A great breath of decay growing by increments, a bit of dead tissue here, a little more pathology over there, until finally all the life had been forced out of it, and all one breathed was death!

The place resembled a morgue in other ways as well. It was cold. The dank chill made the concrete walls sweat with condensation. Lying on the cot, Céline traced words on the walls with a fingernail, then watched his calligraphy trickle to the floor. "If only my books had dissolved like this," he told himself, "I'd be sleeping in a warm bed in Paris!"

As a doctor he'd spent his share of days among the dead. But spending the night—that was something else! Two nights turned into five, five into ten. One morning brought a change. The door swung open; a pair of uniformed guards came in. The dull weight on Céline's heart lifted. He pulled himself to his feet. Perhaps freedom was near! But he'd mistaken the signals. The guards clapped metal cuffs on his wrists, bound his torso in a thick straitjacket. As if he were indeed the dangerous beast his accusers imagined! They guided him through banks of locked doors, then into the back of a police paddywagon. He was piled in among a half dozen similarly bound and handcuffed prisoners.

A tense ride across the city. Police headquarters! Céline found himself in a narrow vertical lockup, a cell shaped like a sentry box. Surely they didn't expect him to stand there long? A man in his fifties! Supposedly the Danes were reasonable men, not sadists. An hour went by, two, three. What about the others? Were they getting the third degree? Finally his turn came. He was led up several flights of stairs, down a dim maze of corridors. By the time he reached the right door he was crumpling at the knees. Yellow light spilled over brown desks. He faced three English-speaking detectives from the Danish national police. The detectives were armed with a dossier of the charges against him, provided by the French ambassador.

He was asked to admit his crimes. How could he? He didn't know what they were! Documents were put before him. He was told to read them over, then sign them. Did he have any choice? No one answered. He began to read.

The documents charged him with multiple counts of collaboration. It was stated that he'd been a member of pro-Nazi organizations. (But he'd never belonged to those organizations!) That he'd had dealings with S.S. officers. (But he'd never heard of those officers!) That wartime writings of his had been acts of treason, welcoming gestures to France's enemy. (But the writings cited were in fact quite innocuous, such as the introduction to a book on local history!) And that he'd delivered statements to the French collaborationist papers. (But hadn't he earned a risky notoriety making fun of those same papers?) The list of charges went on. So one paper, *Le Cri du Peuple,* had quoted him as supporting Doriot in '43? Obviously they'd been using his name for purposes of their own! So another one, *Germinal,* had run an "interview" with him in '44? But they'd merely been eavesdropping, copying down his spoken opinions! And what were those opinions? Let everybody look and see! The *Germinal* piece, he told the Danish police, went no further than what he'd been saying for years: France was suffering from a fatal illness—the illness of money—and was going to give up the ghost soon, unless everybody got together and did the Bolsheviks one better. How? Céline's face broke apart in a cracked smile. By creating a "Supercommunism," an impassioned egalitarianism of the heart! What else had he been talking about in the last of his pamphlets, *Les Beaux Draps*?

The words were rushing out of him now; the police interrogators sat back open-mouthed.

These documents of theirs were a joke! It made his head swim to even try to read through such stuff! Spy, traitor, saboteur, collaborator? He pushed the papers away, threw the pen down.

Lucette, meanwhile, remained in custody less than two weeks. In the women's infirmary, where she was sent after embarking on a hunger strike her first day at Vestre, the other women prisoners, mostly veteran streetwalkers, took her inability to speak Danish as proof she'd been jailed for espionage. They whispered behind her back: *"Sticker!"* If the whores of Vestre Faengsel were recidivists, they were also patriots, it seemed. The Danish word for spy made its way into Lucette's small vocabulary of the language.

The police had no charges against her. She was detained nevertheless, put through hours of questioning. She kept asking her interrogators where her husband was. They refused to disclose Céline's whereabouts, leading her to believe he'd been extradited back to France. If they thought her fear and uncertainty on that score might soften her resolve to defend

him, they were wrong. But—the questioners insisted—Céline had *said* something, hadn't he? *Written* something? He
was an abortionist, wasn't that right? She'd seen this syringe
before, hadn't she? This morphine, this cocaine? This sachet
of belladonna?

All these questions in English confused her. She sat stoically
in handcuffs, shaking her head and frowning. No, none of
it was true, she said at last.

A few days before New Year's she was released from Vestre
Faengsel. She went back to the flat on Ved Stranden. Only
then did she learn that her husband was still in the prison.

On the Feast of the Epiphany—a local holiday and tradi-
tional visiting day at Vestre Faengsel—she went to see him
for the first time. It was a depressing trip, made even gloomier
by the surroundings. The visitors' reception room at Vestre
was a cheerless vault with high ceilings and a lot of divisive
grillwork. Unshaded bulbs hung on wires from ceiling fix-
tures, weighing everything in the room with a grim burden
of shadow.

Ushered in by two guards, Céline stood before her in the
familiar drooping posture that had often brought to people's
minds the stoop of a large ape. The harsh yellowish light of
the reception room, accentuating his large sad eyes and pro-
truding facial bones, made his head look almost like one of
those gaping skulls of early hominids displayed in museums.
The appearance of morbidity was exaggerated by an eye in-
fection, which caused his eyelids to stick together. When he
blinked, the lids fluttered like moths trapped in cobwebs. It
took them a moment to get free. "Luci!" he cried. When

Lucette handed him a red rose she'd brought along, Céline started to sway. "Watch it," one of the guards said to the other in Danish. "He's going to pass out." The second guard signaled to Lucette that she couldn't stay any longer and led the woozy prisoner away.

A week later she came again and was allowed to see him for fifteen minutes. He looked terrible. He wanted to talk nonetheless; in a month of silence, he'd saved up much to say to her. She began to answer in French, but a guard interrupted and told them they could converse only in English. Lucette's English was good enough for everyday practical business, but not for business of the heart. She sat mute as Céline spoke. After ten minutes he complained of a headache. A nervous tremor swept over him, jerking his head to one side. Once the spasm passed, he struggled to rise to his feet, but tottered only a few steps before falling over. The guards helped him up. He required a steadying hand to find his way out.

Lucette ran back to Ved Stranden in dismay. "How long can he survive like this?" she wrote to her mother that night. "Seeing him in this state makes me suffer so!" She'd been trying to control herself, but as she wrote, she abandoned herself to her emotions, weeping large tears onto the thin airmail pages. "My worst fear is that his enemies will come for him, drag him back to France, and that'll be the end!"

She stopped going out. The arrest had cost her all her dance-instruction jobs. She felt as alone and stranded as her husband. He had lost his freedom, she had lost him! What else was there to do but wait? She waited, until her nerves were raw. One day a nasty rash broke out on her hands. The next day it was worse. Her stomach felt jumpy, she lost weight. Time became something she measured in terms of hours and minutes until her next visit to Vestre Faengsel.

On visiting days she did her best to put up a cheerful appearance. She said almost nothing but sat looking with a gaze compounded of love, concern and the sad confusion an animal shows, watching over a wounded mate. That solicitous gaze was sustenance to Céline. Something his soul needed to keep alive!

Though animals weren't allowed into Vestre Faengsel, Lucette managed on several occasions to smuggle in Bébert, curled up and motionless in her bag. When the guards weren't looking, she opened the bag to let her husband peek inside. Céline's eyes lit up with surprise. From the darkness of his nest, Bébert peered up like a phlegmatic oracle.

Back in the cell that was like a morgue, Céline observed his own physical decline with the same attention he'd once have given to the symptoms of a failing patient.

His digestive system, chronically disfunctional as a result of an attack of dysentery in Africa two decades earlier, reacted violently against the dietary regime of Vestre Faengsel; his intestines locked up as tight as his cell door. More alarming, he contracted pellagra, a serious vitamin-deficiency disease. Rare in modern times, this disease, as Céline knew, had once been common among prisoners. Inside this ancient prison, whose depths reminded him so much of a ship's hold, he'd come down with a disease that had once flourished on the penal ships of the Napoleonic era! The pellagra affected his eyes, his skin and his nervous system. Then, too, the damp chill of his cell induced widespread rheumatic pains, most severe in the region of his old war injury, his right arm and shoulder. And he began to suffer migraines so intense that, together with the vertigo resulting from his chronic inner-ear disturbance (also the residue of 1914), they made it difficult for him to stand up.

One day he found himself being lifted by two guards who propped him up with an arm under each of his shoulders and carried him off to the prison infirmary. Doctors there, suspecting that a partially blocked cerebral artery might be causing his terrible headaches, considered surgery to relieve pressure on his brain. They abandoned this plan when it became clear that the patient was responding well to the infirmary regime: vitamin injections, a warm bed, decent meals and—after a few weeks—a little daily exercise in the prison garden.

In the infirmary Céline could breath without feeling he was inhaling the effluvia of a thousand walking corpses. His cell had a window that provided not only ventilation but a view of one of the wings of the prison. It gave him his first good look at the exterior of his new home. Architecturally, Vestre Faengsel had all the charm of an enormous stack of yellow and red bricks. The blocklike three-story structure had been built in a sixteenth-century style one might have termed "imposing": that is, as heavy as the souls of the men trapped inside. Squatting like vultures' nests on its roof peak were the gun turrets, from which dark figures trained automatic weapons down on the prison grounds.

Beyond a high outer wall, a Jewish cemetery, bordered by dark pines and bare silver birches, completed the bleak pan-orama. When Céline looked out on winter mornings, the white headstones were floating like ice wafers atop frosty ground fogs that had rolled in off the Baltic overnight. The distant pale sun, low in the western sky, disappeared behind a wing of the prison shortly past noon every day. Then the graveyard sank into shadow. By midafternoon the Jewish burial ground looked as cold as a marble-and-ivory city on the dark side of the moon. The old sorrows enearthed there had begun to seem to Céline less and less remote from his own.

From the moment of Céline's arrest, French ambassador Charbonnière had been urging the Danish government to extradite him to France, in keeping with a reciprocity agree-ment between the two countries. (The agreement provided that in return for the extradition of Céline, France would surrender a Danish fugitive to Denmark.) The man was a notorious collaborator, said the French ambassador: a dan-gerous criminal, and everyone knew it! Shipping him back to face his punishment would be a simple act of diplomatic good faith between two friendly countries. Nothing could be more straightforward, insisted Charbonnière.

The matter appeared less clear to the Danish foreign office and ministry of justice. Denmark was holding Céline under a law applying to illegal aliens. Because he'd applied for and been granted legal residence status, however, the statute didn't strictly apply to him, and he'd committed no other crime. In fact, only the French demand for extradition was keeping Céline in a Danish prison. And since the French demand was so far based on charges that had not been proven, the Danes were left in a touchy position. Detaining Céline any longer would require a stretching of Danish law; but taking either of the alternative courses—setting him free or extraditing him—was to risk adverse historical judgment. If he was set free, the international political Left would charge Denmark with condoning war crimes. If, on the other hand, he was extradited and then executed, the responsibility for his death might be seen to rest with the Danes. Confronted with this dilemma, the Danish government could come to no clear decision. So Denmark went on dragging its feet. The authorities kept Céline locked up in Vestre Faengsel, but granted him a temporary stay of extradition that had been requested by Thorvald Mikkelsen's legal partner (who was handling the case while Mikkelsen remained on vacation in America).

In one important respect the stay of extradition worked in Céline's favor; it put a little more time between him and the French Courts of Justice. Time was the only thing capable of ameliorating the climate of hatred against him—a climate so heated at this point that it was quite likely to boil up into a death sentence in the event of his return to France.

Not that Céline himself could be expected to endure those dark cold months of early 1946 any better simply because time was passing while he sat shivering in a cell. His taste for American gangster movies had long ago familiarized him with the Hollywood underworld term for the condition of a man who accepts imprisonment to avoid more dangerous forms of retribution. But being "on ice," as the saying went, became less attractive when it threatened to become more than a mere figure of speech: Between periodic thaws, the Denmark he saw from Vestre Faengsel that winter appeared to him for all the world like a glacier, in which he was as permanently immured as some prehistoric fossil.

Céline was shuttled around the blocks and tiers of Vestre Faengsel like a counter on a game board. When at the end of the first week of February the infirmary doctors decided he was fit enough to return to the cell blocks, he was moved again, as usual without any warning.

One cold morning guards conducted him to the west wing of the prison and placed him in a cell in the ground-floor section known as Pavilion K. It was the prison's maximum isolation area, normally reserved for convicted murderers awaiting execution. Céline, the accused war criminal, became Pavilion K's only foreign guest, an honor he soon grew to regard as the worst thing that had ever happened to him.

The single overhead bulb cast a cold halo of shadow on the concrete. He sat on a wooden stool, slowly rocking back and forth. A physician visiting him in his cell would have been quick to note the signs of pellagra. His eyes and hands were swollen, the back of his thin neck speckled with open sores. Nervous tics periodically yanked at his upper body, making his head and shoulders jerk back as if he were being slapped. Wrapped in a blanket, he bent unsteadily over a wooden writing board propped across his lap, muttering to himself and scrawling at intervals with a pencil stub on small sheets of yellow paper.

The condemned killers in the adjacent cells weren't ashamed to share their sleepless anguish with him. Their unhappy, half-crazed howls—calculated, he sometimes suspected, to keep dead victims at bay—were epics of lamentation that poured forward from episode to episode without transition or relief. His inability to understand the Danish language didn't prevent him from comprehending emotionally. The disorganized choral themes of the nocturnal howlers resolved into a simple message: Death was very near, and as it approached, its burden on those who recognized it grew harder and harder to bear.

The peak of the night's delirium usually occurred sometime past midnight, when sirens swelled in a Klaxon din as police paddywagons, returning from a sweep of the city's red-light districts, pulled into the prison yard. Vehicles braked with squealing tires; barred doors banged; guard dogs barked in frenzy. Then voices rang out, as the newly arrested drunks, pimps and streetwalkers were assailed by vice-squad interrogators in an open tank at the bottom of the prison's great well. Weeping, babble, mayhem! The murderers of Pavilion K echoed the whole thing back in a fresh wave of howls, a tortured backwash of bedlam.

The confusing acoustics of Vestre Faengsel warped this din into a single high-decibel roar that rolled across the complicated superstructure of the old jail, like a gale going through the riggings of a prison vessel. With its multiple decks and its hold full of unfortunate men, Vestre was a boat pitched over wild seas by a wind that became a tormenting song, carrying the voices of accusers living and dead.

Letting the writing board slide from his lap to the floor, Céline clapped his hands to his ears and began to yell along with the others.

Morning. He sat rocking on his stool, the writing board across his lap. The cell block was quiet, the condemned men lost in morose daylight broodings. After a while a key jangled in the lock; the heavy cell door swung open. A thickset guard stepped in. Céline looked up; the guard grinned, muttered something unintelligible in Danish. Then he pulled out his pistol, pointed it at the prisoner and cocked it. Stupefied, Céline didn't budge. A brief, tense moment . . . how long? Ten seconds? A minute? Half a lifetime! Suddenly the guard laughed, enjoying his prank. After eyeing Céline to see what effect his cruel pantomime had produced, he left again, slamming the cell door. A few minutes later the grill along the floor slid open; a bowl of porridge was pushed through.

Céline went on writing: "The turnkey's idea of a little joke. *Merde!* But one gets used to it. Oh, yes. Everything—even the looks on their faces. The guards, the cops, all wearing the same smug masks—reflections of the mugs of the vengeance addicts back in France! That look of satisfaction, as though they gained by your death. As though your death and theirs were balanced on scales, tipping another hour of life over to their side every time your death drags you down another hour closer!"

He had nobody to talk to but himself.

Once a day he was let out of his cell and made to walk down one of Vestre Faengsel's many interior passageways, a long corridor with so many unexpected twists he was at first surprised it led anywhere at all. From a series of slits high up in the walls, machine guns followed him all the way. Ahead and behind, iron gates slid open, then shut.

"Automation!" he exclaimed to no one. "A mechanized labyrinth, like what I saw in American slaughterhouses. They drive the poor beasts through, only to end up where? In pools of their own blood! Oh, the humanity of modern science! Industrial miracle! A superefficiency of death! And then they bring on the tour buses, to show off this gleaming techno-logical marvel. And to whom? The same idiots who'll end up poisoned by all that overexcited, hyperadrenalized beef!"

A final door rattled shut behind him. He found himself in a small cell wedged between two walls. Enclosed by iron grillwork instead of bars, the cell was open to the sky. Only two meters by two meters, barely big enough to turn around in: a tiny open-air cage. Light snow was falling. Flakes whirled around inside the cage, slowly piling up on the floor. Céline stood in a snowy vertigo of light, his teeth chattering, his face tilted up to the white sky. Perhaps his vision was failing him, but what he thought he saw when he looked up was the absolute whiteness of eternity.

Mikkelsen's return from America in late March made no immediate impact on Céline's case. It did, however, give him a way to contact Lucette by mail, which he'd been unable to do during his first three months in Vestre Faengsel. Letters that were to pass through the prison censor had to be written in either Danish or English, but client-lawyer correspondence was excepted. Céline's letters in French to Mikkelsen thus came to serve a double function. The opening paragraphs were directed to the lawyer. Then, abruptly, the tone changed as the prisoner began to address his wife.

Mikkelsen let Lucette read the letters in his office but refused to allow her to keep even the pages directed to her. In this way the attorney began to assert influence not only over Céline's legal condition but over his personal affairs.

Céline was in no position to object. He could not act for himself, he had lost power over his own fate, which now rested in the hands of others. The essence of the problem was not legal but metaphysical. Legally, none of it made sense. But in a disordered universe, who could expect laws to make sense? "Oh yes, all this suffering is mathematically perfect, irrefutable in every way," he wrote to Lucette. "Except for one thing. It's all insane. There's no reason for me to be here!"

He wrote long letters every day. To Mikkelsen he would

complain about legal delays, describe the coldness of his cell, ask for wool underwear. To Lucette, in the continuation of the same letter, he would express the less material side of his misery. "I'm reminded," he told her one day, "of that terrible thought of Chateaubriand's: 'Only the unhappy can judge the unhappy, the emotions of prosperity are too gross to comprehend the delicate emotions of distress.' "

In other passages he tried to console his wife by sounding, if not hopeful, at least philosophically resigned. "I do what I'm told and watch what goes on," he told her. "I try to be a model prisoner, and not to let the glacial contempt and moral superiority of my keepers affect me. In their eyes I simply don't exist, and that's how I prefer it. Remember those old paddlewheel steamers? They had a mechanic who did tricks to keep them going. That mechanic never missed a shot. To miss would have cost him his life. He had to climb up on a little platform and oil the big wheel while it was turning. Very delicate, that little trick. He used an oilcan with a long pointed nose, which he had to stick into the hole at exactly the right moment. If he missed, the wheel got him. Being in here is like that. I've got to do everything as though it were a matter of life or death. The smallest thing becomes an impossible trick I've got to make myself perform perfectly, or else I'll get knocked off the deck and chewed up by the big wheel. So I don't let the cage scare me, I read a little, I try to work. And then when I've gone ten days without a bowel movement, and the peeling skin on my backside gets stuck to the wood of my little stool, I just howl a little louder than the other howlers. I imitate a big dog, until they can hear me all the way across the five footbridges and beyond the fourteen crosswalks. Then they come and carry me off to the hospital, where I get to see Irma G., arch-Baltic nurse of nurses, who doses me with her vitamins and hot enemas! One of her enemas is as bad as getting shot up by the Fritz all over again. But I put up with it, because it's my only shot at surviving!"

Determination alone wasn't sufficient to allow Céline to survive Pavilion K. In April he suffered episodes of extreme depression accompanied by severe pains in his back and heart. He returned to the infirmary, where doctors treated him with injections of morphine and vitamin B-12 that eased his physical symptoms. His spirits continued to sink. How long would the reprieve last this time? Any day might see him back in a cell block. Thinking about it brought him so low that the refuge of death, as he wrote to Lucette in mid-June, now seemed "a sweet asylum."

Her own life was far from easy. That summer, when Karen Jensen suddenly returned from Spain, Lucette was left homeless. She found a small attic apartment on Kronprincessegade—an "artist's garret" under the roofs. For living expenses she depended on monthly handouts from Karen, who along with Hella Johansen continued to manage what was left of Céline's gold.

·　·　·

Céline had learned from his patients in Clichy that circumstances sometimes made it wiser to stay ill than to face the consequences of being healthy. In his Clichy patients' case the issue was avoiding work; in his own it was avoiding a return to the "death row" of Vestre Faengsel. But by August there was no more avoiding it. He was well enough to get around, which meant he could be transferred back to a cell block. The guards who slowly walked him back to Pavilion K looked apologetic when they locked him up.

After another month among the murderers, he was sicker than ever. Pellagra made his hands and feet swell so badly he could neither walk nor grip a pencil without pain. Once again the disease brought on skin lesions and waves of nervous tremors. Headaches and intestinal pains turned his nights into hallucinations. No longer able to watch his suffering without a pang of conscience, the guards appointed a trustee to the job of sweeping and scrubbing his cell; the prisoner clearly couldn't do it for himself.

Mikkelsen came to see him and got a shock. If the lawyer had ever doubted the reality of Céline's complaints, one glance at him in the visitors' room dispelled them. The author of *Death on the Installment Plan* looked as if he had very few payments left to make.

Concerned about his client's state, Mikkelsen appealed directly to the Danish minister of foreign affairs, arguing that the French-Danish extradition treaty didn't apply in Céline's case. He was not a convicted criminal but a political refugee, said Mikkelsen, and a sick man to boot; as such he deserved not extradition but freedom, protection and asylum, in keeping with the liberal traditions of Denmark.

The minister's reply was predictably equivocal: The Danish government would go on delaying extradition as a matter of principle, but before Céline could be released his medical condition would have to be confirmed through the ministry of justice. Dutifully shifting his attention from ministry to ministry, Mikkelsen applied for and obtained the medical confirmation. But another month went by, and Céline looked thinner and weaker than ever. The lawyer anxiously redirected his efforts to the Copenhagen police. In a strongly worded letter, he charged that endless legal delays were resulting in cruel and unnecessary hardship for the prisoner, who was now in danger of dying in Vestre Faengsel—an eventuality that would be very embarrassing for Denmark.

The letter had its effect. By late September gears were turning inside the Danish legal machine, preparing Céline's release. At this point, however, French ambassador Charbonnière, a man already much hated by Céline (who spent long hours dreaming up insulting variants on the spelling of his name), managed once again to throw a wrench into the works. He presented the Danish minister of justice with a new set of treason charges, accusing Céline of promulgating anti-Semitism in his prewar writings; of slandering a Jewish doctor in one of his pamphlets; of honorary membership in the European Circle, a German propaganda association; and of fleeing to Germany in 1944. Until this document could be studied by the Danes, Céline would remain a prisoner of international diplomacy.

Mikkelsen supplied a copy of Charbonnière's statement to his client in Pavilion K. Céline summoned the energy to annotate its margins, writing angrily alongside each charge, "Lie!" "Lie!" "Absolutely false!"

On October 19 he was driven again from Vestre Faengsel to police headquarters. Another round of questioning, this time with Mikkelsen present. Céline—now reduced to a handcuffed ghost of himself—shakily rebutted all the French government's allegations. Back in his cell he requested pen and paper. Writing in an indignant frenzy interrupted only by long pauses to catch his breath, he composed an angry seventeen-page "defense" which he sent to Mikkelsen. Along with the "defense" he enclosed a brief personal note to the lawyer, terming the French charges "an idiotic jumble of lies, surmises and gibberish."

The first point of his "defense" was disingenuous—an emphatic denial that he'd ever advocated the persecution of Jews. While this was technically the truth, it was the kind of statement that answered a legal charge only at the cost of raising moral questions far more serious—for if his prewar pamphlets hadn't advocated persecution, they had certainly helped create the atmosphere of racial hatred in which, later, many "decent" French citizens had looked on dispassionately as their Jewish neighbors were herded off to the camps.

More convincingly, he maintained in this "defense" that during the war he had refused all pressures exerted to make him work as a propagandist for the enemy; that both the Vichy government and the Germans had seized and suppressed his books; and that he'd even been attacked in the

S.S. paper *Schwartze Korps* and in Goebbels' book *Das Reich*! As a matter of fact, he added defiantly, there'd even been a time during the war when with the slightest of acquiescence on his part he'd have been appointed as High Commissioner for the Jewish Question! The temptation to accept had been hard to resist, but he had declined the post. For that act of grace alone the Jews ought to have erected a statue in his honor—out of gratitude for all the harm he *hadn't* done them, though he'd had the chance!

He was charged, further, with taking refuge in Germany at the war's end. Just think of it! When all the time he'd been doing his best to get *out* of Germany! Germany—a country he'd always detested! Germany—where he and his wife had been treated as badly as pigs, and fed even worse!

In addition to the bravado and flamboyance familiar to readers of his pamphlets, the "defense" contained a liberal dose of the imaginative immoderation for which his novels were famous. He denied, for instance, that he'd ever met the Third Reich's ambassador to France, then undercut this dis- avowal by adding that as much as he'd disliked Otto Abetz, he'd considered Abetz's wife even more disgusting!

Aggressive about his innocence on paper, Céline was none- theless pessimistic about his chances of forestalling extradi- tion. Expecting to be sent back to France any day, he sent a personal note, written in his best English, to the chief of police. In it he asked to be allowed to see Lucette one last time. "My future as I make out looks gloomy," he told the police chief. "At the end I feel I will be given to the French police. To meet my wife therefore would be a great relief, as probably once in the hands of the French police (which works now very much on the Russian pattern) we will probably never meet again until death." He also requested to be sent to a hospital, so he could regain his strength before facing the legal struggle ahead of him in France.

Mikkelsen presented the Danish ministry of justice with an edited version of Céline's defense. Two days later, on November 8, 1946, Céline was taken out of his cell and helped to an ambulance that waited at the gates of the prison. It carried him across the city to a large old building in a residential neighborhood, Sundby Hospital. The guards who escorted him into the private hospital were carrying guns, but Céline couldn't have escaped if he'd wanted to. He was a very sick man, barely able to walk.

From the relative comfort of Sundby, the wild nights in Pavilion K seemed less a memory than a bad dream to Céline. He tried to forget them, to concentrate on the present. A drastic change in diet helped. With the easing of his intestinal symptoms, his appetite returned. He marveled to find placed before him such unlikely objects as an orange or a tomato, objects as rare as manna inside Vestre Faengsel—or, for that matter, in any place he'd been since leaving Paris.

Within a few weeks he'd regained the strength to read and write for several hours at a stretch without exhausting himself. Sitting up in bed with a writing board on his lap, he went over the small tablets of scribblings he'd done at Vestre, beginning the arduous task of re-casting them into a novel.

As he worked, a police guard, charged with keeping watch over the prisoner, sat idly in a chair just outside the room. Looking up from his papers, Céline's glance wandered out toward the corridor, where, framed in the doorway, the square-toed uniform shoes of the guard were visible: a silent reminder that the French ambassador hadn't forgotten the "Céline affair."

"Charbonnière!" Céline scrawled on the tablet in his lap. "I'm essential to his career. How else can he fabricate the credentials of a Resistance hero? My case is made to order for him. Dragging me back for trial, that'll stand as proof of his retroactive heroics! He may have spent the whole war ducking under a desk, but now that it's over he has a chance to demonstrate his bravery in a much less dangerous fashion—by hounding a sick man to death!"

If the ambassador was thinking about Céline, he evidently wasn't alone. Thanks to the French left-wing press, the extradition of the "Monster of Montmartre" became more of a cause célèbre every day.

Appearing at the hospital one morning with a selection of the latest French periodicals, Mikkelsen wore the embarrassed expression of a delivery boy who knows the package he's about to hand you contains something unpleasant.

Céline propped himself up on two pillows and leafed swiftly through the pages of newsprint. Slowing down to note passages the lawyer had marked, he commented under his breath, displaying first impatience, then anger, then disgust. Finally he tossed the papers down in a disordered splash on the coverlet.

"*Merde!* Once they put a price on your neck, they don't care how scrawny it gets! Instead of forgiveness, it's 'all right, hold still,' and then *whoop!*" Flattening his left hand into the shape of a blade, Céline let it drop onto the sheets. "Off comes the head!"

Mikkelsen folded the newspapers and placed them in a neat stack at the foot of the bed, then took out his pipe and began filling it from a leather pouch. "Give them time, they'll forget you."

"Forget? Never!" Céline's voice rang like a gunshot down the hospital corridor. "They've been out to get me for ten years—ever since I had the nerve to tell the truth about Russia in *Mea Culpa*. Ten years of being trailed by a gang of sadists in shit-stained pants!"

The lawyer struck a match and lit his pipe. He looked away, studying the room's only window. The bare upper limbs of a beech tree were scraping against the glass, stirred by a brisk wind that rattled the pane slightly but didn't penetrate the snug hospital room. After a moment he extracted some documents from his briefcase and began leafing through them.

Céline laughed suddenly. "Ah, Mik, I know it made you nervous, my defense!"

Mikkelsen turned back to him, looking sheepish. "I've told you, I toned it down only where absolutely necessary."

"Spoken like an editor! Now that Denoël's gone, I need a new one, is that it?"

The lawyer blushed. "Of course, I'd never presume—"

Céline cut him off. "This isn't literature, Mik, it's real life. There's no time for halfhearted apologies. My books are blacklisted in France . . . a year in the slammer . . . they've auctioned off my mother's bed, robbed me blind, ten million in cash while I rotted in the hole . . . set fire to my manuscripts, thrown them in the trash!"

"Yes . . ." The lawyer tamped his pipe.

"They wipe the shit from their boots off on me in the papers. . . . Why? Out of pure hatred! The pleasure of vengeance! An abstraction! Just to fuck me over for sport! Dogs playing with the corpse of a rabbit!" Céline stopped to get his breath.

"What's the point of rehearsing all this?"

"You believe in justice," Céline went on, quieter now. "So you don't want any evidence of men's dirty tricks spoiling your lunch. Me, I *expect* the French to behave like this. I've come to know what they're like. They'd betray their own countryman, if it was of use to them—and then sell the wind that blows over his grave."

Mikkelsen shook his head. "I admit, you've suffered . . ." His voice trailed off. He turned away, staring out the window again. Snow had begun to fall. Tiny flakes blew against the window, bounced off like startled midges, then swirled away on the wind. A nurse came in and filled the patient's water pitcher, then bustled out, wishing Mikkelsen a brusque good afternoon in Danish.

Céline stirred in bed, rolling his eyes. "Pleasant, aren't they? I'm an important person here. Clearly they think I'm an enemy agent of some kind!"

Mikkelsen laughed, relieved by the return of his client's sense of humor. "They're taking good care of you, I see."

"Perhaps too good. I must be careful not to recuperate too quickly."

"But it's only been two weeks."

"I'd be happy to stay two months—two years! Whatever you can arrange! In here at least the assassins can't get at me." Céline glanced toward the door. The shoes of the guard sitting outside could still be seen sticking out like disembodied sentinels. "But they won't leave me in peace for long. The pampering of sacrificial animals is always temporary. You know, I'm like a horse in the Spanish *corrida*. They fill his belly, treat him like royalty, but only so he can come back to the *corrida*!"

The long hours of inactivity at Sundby gave Céline plenty of opportunity to reflect. He let his mind's eye wander at random through the past, summoning up people he'd known and might never see again. His family, old friends, lovers, dancers. It was a shock when in the middle of his daydreams, one of those dancers turned up at Sundby.

It was Karen Jensen. When she walked into his hospital room, Céline, lost in reverie, thought at first he was seeing a ghost. But Karen was very much alive, and no less lovely than he remembered her—a tall, shapely brunette, whose finely chiseled cheek bones and large, sensuous mouth, accentuated by dark lipstick, brought the past back to Céline with such vivid force it was as if he were momentarily young again. She handed him a bouquet of wild flowers, picked at Hella's country place, and kissed him affectionately. "My brave cavalier," she said. "I knew they couldn't kill you."

Karen spent an hour at his side. After she'd talked for a while about her experiences in Spain, they reminisced about happier times in the 1930s, when she had been the toast of his Montmartre circle—a beautiful but unattainable ice princess. Céline teased her about his friend Gen Paul, who'd once wanted to sleep with her. Karen laughed happily, remembering. Then Céline told her he'd heard Gen Paul was now denying any association with him. Karen's face showed genuine surprise. "Don't be shocked," he said. "You'll soon find I'm no longer somebody one's proud to know."

"Ridiculous!" Karen smiled, dismissing his implication. She changed the subject, talking gaily on. But when he asked her how Lucette was getting along, she stopped smiling, as though it displeased her to be reminded that another dancer had eclipsed her in his affections. She hesitated for a minute, and then spilled out a sorry tale about how Lucette, having run up big bills at several shops, had started asking her for extra money well before the end of each month. His gold was disappearing at an alarming rate, Karen said. She went on to itemize all Lucette's "extravagant" purchases.

Listening to the details, Céline grew more and more irate. The idea that Lucette was thoughtlessly exhausting their life savings!

After Karen left, his anger boiled over. He wrote a vicious, accusative letter to his wife.

A few days later Lucette appeared at the hospital—hollow-eyed, her face drawn and streaked with tear tracks. Without waiting for her to speak, Céline let his anger flash out in a full-scale verbal assault. She'd hear such tirades many times—but rarely directed at her.

"While I'm stuck in here," he roared, "what do you do? Throw away my money on nothing! Let it slip through your fingers like water through a net!"

His eyes bulged; saliva trickled from the corners of his mouth.

Sitting quietly beside his bed, Lucette waited for him to tire himself out. Her silence, however, only seemed to intensify his fury.

"I've had enough! I'm going to ask them to send me back to France! Anything! They can bury me in shit if they want to! This can't go on! I'll write to the minister of justice, tell him I'm ready to leave as soon as he can set it up!"

Stung by his threat, Lucette began to cry. The words burst out between sobs—she hadn't spent money on herself; she'd been buying gifts for friends, people who'd tried to help with their legal case. . . .

Céline cut her short.

"Don't make excuses! You're pillaging our future for vats of French perfume! Tropical fruit! Karen's told me all about it. Imported flowers! Fur coats! You'd pass over a dying man for a basket of strawberries! Karen tells me . . ."

"Karen! What do you really know about Karen?"

Céline paused, scrutinizing his wife.

She wiped tears from her eyes. "Perhaps I've been too generous. But how do you know Karen's telling you the truth?" Lucette rummaged through her purse and took out a small notebook, in which she'd kept a detailed record of the payments Karen had made to her. She thrust it at Céline. "See for yourself!"

He looked at the figures for a minute or two, then flushed. His anger lit on a new target. "These Danes! You can't trust them! They've been salting away something for themselves. . . . Karen and Hella—our good friends! They're nothing but blue flies sucking off our plate!"

Lucette's convincing performance at the hospital won her an acquittal in the court of Céline's mind, where judgments were always swift and intuitive. He summoned the two Danish women to the hospital, where, in Lucette's presence and with Mikkelsen on hand as referee, he charged them with mismanaging his money. The meeting turned into a ferocious squabble among the three women, with accusations flying in every direction. Céline told everyone to leave—but asked Mikkelsen to return for a word in private. It was tempting the devil to leave money with women, he told the lawyer; he had made up his mind—he would turn the gold over to him for safekeeping.

Mikkelsen agreed to take charge. He would make twice-monthly payments of 350 crowns in Danish currency to Lucette. Céline signed a receipt acknowledging a debt to the lawyer of 8,400 crowns, representing a year's payments. No record of the gold was committed to paper; in the eyes of anyone who might later examine all this, the payments would appear as a loan from Mikkelsen to Céline. A jeweler friend of Céline's in Paris would give a better exchange rate than could be obtained in the north. Mikkelsen would exchange the gold for currency through the jeweler on visits to Paris. "Do it drop by drop," Céline told him. "And watch out for holes in the boat . . . that golden egg is all I've got left in this world!"

He also gave the lawyer specific orders to resist any effort by Karen or Hella—*or* by Lucette—to alter their financial agreement.

"Pay absolutely no attention to feminine intervention, however friendly and well intended. I don't discuss anything serious with women. I'm obliged to appear to be full of respect and consideration for them, that's all."

Céline never spoke to Karen Jensen again. She rejoined all the other dancers in his ballet of ghosts.

Before Christmas the respite at Sundby came to an end, somewhat sooner than Céline had hoped. Once again he was bound up and put into the back of a police van. As he was driven across the city to Vestre Faengsel, he felt a chill, foul breath on the back of his neck. Death getting closer and closer!

After the warmth and comfort of Sundby, getting used to the frozen cell blocks of Vestre was not easy for Céline. The bleak prospect of having to endure another winter in prison loomed like an unscalable wall in front of his mind. He couldn't think his way past it. "What anguish I feel over being returned to Vestre," he wrote to Lucette. "Such anguish that I'm literally incapable of reasoning."

He received a biographical questionnaire circulated by an American publication called *Who's Important in Literature*. Forwarded from Paris by his former secretary, the questionnaire had taken almost a year to reach him. Not that that was surprising. Considering how far outside the literary world he now found himself, mail from there may as well have been sent to him from another solar system. Supplying answers to the questionnaire was an act that required an equivalent leap of the imagination. Lost on the dark edge of the universe, how did you describe your "Residence" or your "Hobby or Special Interest"? In the first blank, Céline scrawled "Copenhagen Prison"; in the second, "Get out of prison."

The first cold nights of the new year yawned open like dark mouths of insanity. Each morning it was harder for the prisoner to get around. By the morning of the tenth of January, he could not move from a sitting position on the small wooden stool in his cell. How long did they expect him to go on like this? He rocked the stool . . . it toppled over. A guard looked in and saw him lying on the cold floor. He was taken away to the infirmary.

A full medical examination was ordered. Three weeks back in Vestre Faengsel had undone all the good effects of Sundby. Céline now weighed twenty-five pounds less than he had at the date of his arrest, thirteen months before. He suffered from constant headaches, cardiovascular spasms, auditory hallucinations, insomnia, vertigo, back pains, rheumatic pains in his right shoulder and arm, pain and swelling in his right hand, a tachycardiac heart, gastroenteritis, mycosis and pellagra. He had trouble focusing his eyes, exhibited extreme weakness and depression, and was unable to stand up. Most of his teeth had fallen out, and those that remained were so loose he had extreme difficulty chewing.

It took him a month in the infirmary to get back on his feet. During that time, his rage against his Danish jailers flared up in small fits of temper as ineffectual as they were intense. When Mikkelsen came to see him he snarled like a caged beast. "What right do these cretins have to throw my days to the pigs, in this garbage dump of a prison?"

Every day he spent in Vestre Faengsel now seemed to him fresh evidence of the malice of destiny. On February 13, with a return to the cell blocks once again just around the corner, he wrote to the lawyer, for the first time seriously proposing to accept extradition to France. "I think we've played out the comedy, mouthed all the speeches, acted out all the stock gestures. It's time to change the theater! Enough!"

The following day he took matters in his own hands and wrote in English to the Danish national police, complaining that despite getting "twenty promises of liberty," he was still very much in custody. His letter demanded "very respectfully and humbly" that he "be sent back *immediately* to France, absolutely and without delay." His year in prison had made him a "very ill man," he said. "I regret that I do not enjoy the health of a Karlsberg horse, but I am only a poet, a writer, a doctor of medicine . . . my wife also is not a truck horse but an artist . . . and prison is killing me."

In his desperation, Céline was growing increasingly impatient with Mikkelsen's failure to rescue him from Vestre Faengsel. How could a man who seemed to spend all his time wining and dining, smoking and drinking, ever get any legal business done?

But Mikkelsen was doing his best. He continued to pressure the authorities for Céline's release. To support this cause, he presented an international artists' petition, signed by such figures as the French composer Edgar Varèse and American writers Henry Miller, Kenneth Patchen and Edmund Wilson. The petition put forward three main points: That it was unjust for Céline to be punished for his *opinions,* when there was no proof of treasonous *action* on his part; that his only "crime" was the expression of unpopular ideas; and that the charges against him had probably been instigated by his literary enemies in France. Mikkelsen attached to the petition a letter of his own to the minister of justice, in which he pointed out that the United States had refused to extradite Camille Chautemps, a former Vichy minister who'd been sentenced to death in absentia by France. Chautemps, it seemed, was now living unhampered in Washington, D.C.

At last the Danish government acted. Céline would be released from prison for transfer to a state hospital, where he would remain under surveillance.

On February 26, 1947, the prisoner saw his last of Vestre Faengsel. His good-byes to his "residence" of fourteen months were extremely perfunctory. Once again he was taken off in an ambulance. This one carried him through the icy streets of the capital to the Rigshospital, or National Hospital of Copenhagen.

His release from Vestre came none too soon to suit Céline. From somewhere in the outer circles of hell he'd been suddenly transported to what he was soon calling "a paradise" of "silence, calm, felicity, discretion." At the Rigshospital there were no guards. He was free to wander the halls and grounds. Lucette could visit him every day, instead of just once a week. And his mail, for the first time in over a year, was not censored. Céline could correspond freely and privately with lawyers in France.

In April he wrote to a well-known Paris lawyer, Albert Naud, who had defended Pierre Laval against charges of collaboration, and asked him to take on his case. Naud began to look into the French government's "Céline dossier."

Little local comment had attended Céline's first year of imprisonment in Denmark. In April 1947, while he was in the national hospital, that situation changed suddenly. The Danish Communist daily *Land og Folk* (*Nation and People*) inaugurated a series of sternly editorializing articles decrying the presence in Denmark of the infamous fugitive. Largely adapted from French left-wing journals, the articles portrayed Céline as "pro-Nazi," a collaborator and war criminal, and contained hints that he was being treated much too kindly in the national hospital. Céline reacted like a man who'd been hit by lightning, not just once, but several times. Eventually you had to learn to expect it, almost see it coming!

The key "evidence" cited in the stories was a pro-Nazi manifesto allegedly signed by Céline in 1942—which, Céline angrily informed Mikkelsen, was an "absolute forgery"—fabricated either by the Nazis or the Communists, he wasn't sure which. "One of these little shit-diggers, a Danish 'journalist,' went all the way to the offices of *l'Humanité* to dig up this filth. Really, I'd need three secretaries to track down all the falsehoods currently being circulated in my name. Next they'll invent a classic theft of the Eiffel Tower and say I'm to blame!"

Within six weeks of the first *Land og Folk* article, twenty-five doctors at the Rigshospital joined their chief of staff in demanding that the government remove the "pro-Nazi" writer from the institution.

The Danish foreign minister and the French ambassador conferred. What was there to do with this man everyone hated? Nobody had anything to gain from sending him back to Vestre Faengsel. In prison he'd probably die within six months. The French ambassador, resigned to the fact that extradition wasn't imminent, finally agreed to have Céline released from custody, to reside in Copenhagen under the eye of the Danish police.

On June 24, 1947, Céline was discharged from the national hospital, "on his word of honor" not to leave Denmark; at

home he was still charged with violating article seventy-five—
the treason section—of the French penal code.

He went to live with Lucette in her attic apartment on
Kronprincessegade. "I'm here among the wood lice, alas!"
he wrote to friends in France. "With this arrest warrant still
on my tail . . ."

5.
ELSINORE

The summer passed like a season in a dream. Lucette went back to work as a dance instructor. Céline, meanwhile, began a slow re-entry to the world. A year and a half of institutional captivity had ended; but if he was once again a free man, he was also a broken one. The spiritual effects of what he'd been through showed in his dazed, half-open eyes, whose lonely fixity was that of a mechanical clown coming apart at the hinges. His wasted legs poked up thin and bony through baggy gabardine pants; his spindly wrists were lost in the broad, slashed sleeves of the thick woolen work shirts he wore.

That fall he sat for hours on end in a rocking chair, huddled before a small coal fire, surrounded by disordered piles of unwashed clothing—stockings on a table, trousers crumpled on a chair, a nightshirt spilled across a gaping dresser drawer. Loose manuscript pages, covered with his sloping scrawl, filled baskets littered on the floor around his makeshift work desk. What was the use of keeping order in a permanently suspended life?

From France Céline received a copy of Jean-Paul Sartre's "Reflections on the Jewish Question," wherein he found himself portrayed not only as the classic psychological prototype of the anti-Semite, but as a Gestapo agent. "If Céline was able to support the social theory of the Nazis," Sartre had written, "it's because he was paid." The suggestion that he'd prostituted his opinions for money sent Céline into a frenzy. His literary independence, in which he took great pride, had never before been questioned.

To Lucette, Mikkelsen and a few loyal correspondents in France, he exploded against this new archenemy. "An untalented opportunist," he called Sartre. "He was never anything else. When my books were popular with the left, he and Aragon were constantly trying to kiss my ass. Now things have changed, and he's appointed himself judge and hangman in one fell swoop! Myopic little tapeworm that he is! Where was he when the blood was flowing? I'll tell you! Crawling through the intestines of the victors, as he does now! Putting on his 'existentialist' plays for the Kraut intellectuals in Paris! Little shit addict that he is! And now I'm to be bumped off for his lies? 'Paid by the Nazis'! How would he know? Did he peek into the ambassador's checkbook while

Abetz was buggering him? This false little worm of shit, this tadpole of turds! So he's after a mouthful of my blood? All right, then! Let him have it! Blood on draft, in the absolute futurist bar!''

Ignoring the advice of Mikkelsen and his friends in France, who pointed out that responding to Sartre's attack might be risky, Céline poured all his anger into a scathing little essay that made Sartre's piece sound inoffensive in comparison. So Sartre had made him a textbook example of the Jew hater? Well, then, he would reply in kind!

Lacking access to a typist, he copied the piece out by hand. Then there was the question of who was to publish it. No one had published Céline in years. But a certain prominent editor in Paris, whom he'd never met, had recently demonstrated friendly interest in his case. Céline's private nickname for this editor was ''clancul''—from *clanculus,* a mollusk that takes on the properties of the rocks where it's found. Still, the editor had invited him to write something about his case, and had even offered to break the blacklist by publishing it. Céline decided to send the anti-Sartre piece to him. He mailed it off. But as time went by it became apparent the editor was going to live up to Céline's nickname. He wrote back praising Céline's obscene satire, but refrained from publishing it.

Céline wasn't really surprised. The wave of hatred against him was still building. While that was going on, he couldn't expect to find any real allies. ''The wave will crest someday,'' he told Lucette. ''Perhaps in ten years—no sooner. And when it does . . . the keys of Lady Macbeth will open some curious doors!"

He felt betrayed by everyone—his "Aryan brothers" most of all.

"As for the Jewish Question," he wrote to a supporter in France, "you can't imagine how much sympathy I feel for Jews after seeing the Aryans at work! The Fritz and the French, they've both proven themselves to be filthy packs of apes— nothing but brutes, flunkies, whores and swindlers. No pride, no loyalty, no balls! But the Jews—I've come to an under- standing with them. They alone are curious, inquisitive, mystical, messianic! After my own style! The Jews' only crime was their hysteria. Mine also! And they have paid, as I'm doing now. But my Aryan brothers? They're rolling in the aisles. To them I'm just a sideshow act—the 'Monster of Montmartre'! I wanted to save them from the slaughterhouse. I should have saved my breath. The Jews at least have the excuse of an emotion directed to a cause, an idea, a passion. The Aryans' only excuse is a tune, a meal or the Legion of Honor! So for God's sake, long live the Jews! I'd go to Tel Aviv if they allowed me. Why not? It'd be a pleasure. That's where I belong."

In October Mikkelsen proposed an outing to Elsinore, one of the many Danish historical sites he'd long tried to persuade

Céline to visit. As usual, Céline wasn't keen on the idea, but Lucette wanted to go—she pointed out they'd seen almost nothing of the country—and Mikkelsen was adamant. "Walk where Prince Hamlet walked, on his own journey to the end of the night," he bantered with Céline.

On the appointed day, Céline began the trip in a sour humor. He sulked in the back seat.

A gray morning sky closed in over the road that hugged the coast as it curved northward. The beech forests of the big estates along the Sound had a spectral look. There were some trees that still held autumn's eerie glow in a few golden leaves, but a larger part of the woods appeared somber and brooding. The silence in the car seemed an extension of the silence in the forest's interior.

"Lovely, isn't it?" Mikkelsen prompted over his shoulder as he drove.

"Something Gothic about those woods," Céline grumbled from the rear. "As if Andersen's huntsmen were in there, violating Snow White."

Lucette, riding in front, turned and laughed.

"All this was oak once." The lawyer indicated a nearby stand of leafless beech trees. "Well before Andersen's time— the oak of the great sailing ships. But then, when they stopped building wooden ships, everything was re-planted. These beeches make better firewood than oak."

"The practical race of Danes," Céline said, "with their profitable forests!"

"Also beautiful," Lucette said diplomatically.

"You ought to see them in the spring," Mikkelsen nodded.

"Keeping up these forests has been more a labor of love than of profit. The new landowners all want to put in spruce or larch. The last few years, all you hear is talk of 'faster forests.' "

"Quicker cash!" Céline put in. "A common attitude everywhere, since the war."

At a scenic spot Mikkelsen parked by the road. Spires of smoke rose out of the surrounding woods like gray smudges of gouache on tissue paper. From nearby trees the doleful monotone cry of a cuckoo floated through the air. Mikkelsen unpacked a lunch. Over paté, sardines and a white French wine, the voluble attorney regaled them with an exposition of Danish forestry, agriculture and animal husbandry. Céline refused to drink the wine and punctuated Mikkelsen's conversation with acerbic comments. When the sandwiches were gone, they got back in the car and continued north.

In early afternoon they reached Elsinore. The huge brick and sandstone castle jutted out on a rocky promontory into the Sound, only three miles from Sweden. Below its battlements the waters of the Baltic stretched out flat and cold. Beyond lay the yellow cliffs of the Swedish coast, their outlines broken up in pale bluish spray. Fishing birds swooped down through strands of mist with shrieks that rent the air like metal being torn. Clouds streamed in off the water, masking the castle's green copper roofs.

Mikkelsen dallied at the main gate to deliver a little speech as prelude, tracing the Hamlet story all the way back to Saxo Grammaticus and the *Historia Danica,* until at length Céline broke in impatiently. "Brevity is the soul of wit, Mik!"

The lawyer led Céline and Lucette on a tour through the castle, ending up on the windy platform of the Flag Battery, among rows of rusty archaic guns and pyramids of bronze cannonballs turning green with age. The whitecapped breakers of the Sound bucked up over a stone retaining wall only a few meters away. As each wave was sucked back into the undertow, a lacy rinse of foam sloshed against the ramparts.

"This is the platform on which Hamlet met his father's ghost." Mikkelsen raised a hand to his mouth to block out the wind, which was blowing hard across the exposed stone terrace. " 'In the same figure, like the King that's dead . . .' "

Céline braced himself to keep from being blown over. "This place makes Hamlet's depression quite plausible," he shouted back into the wind. "No wonder he thought about nothing but revenge! He spent too much time alone in Denmark!"

Mikkelsen didn't reply. They stood a moment longer, gazing at the wind-whipped water.

Céline made an abrupt sweeping gesture with his bad right hand and intoned a single line in perfect theatrical English: "A sea to fish for souls . . ."

His voice was lost in wind noise and the cries of gulls.

If, like Hamlet, Céline thought "Denmark's a prison," he could at least move around within its confines. In fact, he soon had to.

The owner of the Kronprincessegade flat informed Céline

and Lucette that he planned to re-occupy it in the spring. Housing in Copenhagen was costly and hard to find. Céline talked the problem over with Mikkelsen, who proposed a solution. The lawyer said he had a country property consisting of a summerhouse and several small cottages at Klarskovgaard, a remote outpost on the west coast of Seeland. He offered to put up the couple there. It was a long way from Paris—it was a long way from *anywhere*—but Céline had run out of choices.

"We're going to get out of Copenhagen," he wrote to a correspondent in France. "Life's too expensive here, and our miserable savings are running out. So it's off to the country, which I hate, and specifically the coast of the Baltic, that sea of cadavers. . . ."

6.
KLARSKOVGAARD

He looked up and down the deserted cobblestone street. Rows of neat cottages with thatched roofs and white plaster walls lined both sides. At one end of the street the docks of the small port of Korsør were visible. Beyond, a patch of open sea changed in color from bleak gray blue to a glittering light green and back again as clouds broke, then re-formed in front of the sun. The only sounds were the cries of curlews overhead and occasional toots coming from the port—the whistle of a ferryboat loading for its trip across the Grand Belt.

Letting out an exaggerated sigh, Céline shouldered his rucksack, planted his stick on the cobbles and began propelling himself forward. Soon he'd achieved the swaying, shuffling gait that was his normal pace. With Bébert nestled in a sack slung around his neck, and in an overlarge topcoat that went almost down to his ankles, he gave what might have passed for a clown's impression of the Wandering Jew. At his side, Lucette, with her erect carriage and dancer's poise, appeared less his companion than his keeper.

A half-mile from the port they found the Korsør police station; Mikkelsen had given them instructions to register there. In hesitant English, the local police chief spelled out the conditions of their residence in the area. After that, his English seemed to break down completely. He made a phone call to summon a taxi for them, then wished them a brusque good day.

The taxi, a large American sedan, had seen better days. Once the driver understood where Céline wanted to go, he frowned and said he didn't like to use that road in bad weather—it wasn't paved. Céline pointed at the sky: Wasn't the weather good today? The driver glanced up doubtfully at the puffy white clouds scudding across a blue backdrop. As he looked, the sky suddenly became overcast again. He shook his head. Céline pulled a handful of *kroner* out of his pocket and began bargaining.

Minutes later he and Lucette were in the back of the battered taxi, bumping through the side streets of Korsør. The road ran along the harbor, then followed low tumbling shoreline dunes. They passed an old wooden lighthouse, a few small farms, a thin red cow or two; after that, nothing. The coastal plain stretched out in an unvarying sandy-yellow ex-

panse, chalk white in places where morning frost still dusted
a patch of moss or tree stump. The travelers noticed ice slicks
lining the inside rims of ruts in the muddy road. Before long
the driver got stuck in one particularly deep furrow, spinning
his wheels intermittently for several minutes before the big
car lurched free of the mud to slither a little further down
the road.

Five miles outside Korsør the terrain began to undulate
slightly, hayfields dipping off toward the sea in a mild slope
on one side, climbing to stands of brush and sparse woods
on the other. Soon the neatly cultivated fields were divided
by boxwood hedgerows, clusters of lilac just coming into
flower and rows of ornamental shrubs. Under the hedgerows
the sandy ochre soil was brightened by spring blooms—pale
yellow primroses, deep blue and purple hyacinths, and waxy
white anemones.

They'd come to a large property bordered to the east and
west by beeches and evergreens. Its several substantial buildings were all in the same whitewashed farmhouse style, with
deep red wooden cross beams and green-gray thatched roofs.
An apple orchard tucked between the main buildings presented a showy array of white blossoms. To the south, several
hundred meters away, some smaller structures were partially
blocked from sight by a dark bank of pines, beneath which
the land dropped off in uneven cliffs to the slate-blue Baltic.

The driver veered off onto a rugged track that led toward
the big thatched house at the front of the estate.

"Klarskovgaard," he said, grinding his gears.

A solid-looking gray-haired man, his cheeks ruddy with

work and weather, was trimming a hedge in front of the main house. He stopped what he was doing and stood watching the taxi approach, hailing the driver with a smile. His face became neutral when he greeted Céline and Lucette. "My name is Petersen," he said, extending a hand to each of the newcomers. "I take care of this place." He looked Céline squarely in the eye, as if assessing the character of a man with whom he was about to enter into business; then he bent and began removing luggage from the taxi.

Lucette released Bébert from his bag to investigate their new surroundings. The old cat poked his nose into the bushes where the caretaker had been working. Petersen, standing with a suitcase in each hand, looked down and measured him with the same unsmiling regard he'd shown the human visitors.

Céline and Lucette were put in the big house, Mikkelsen's own residence. In preparation for the owner's return from a holiday in France, the centuries-old house had been recently cleaned and painted; its windows were flung open to air out the rooms. With the caretaker showing the way, Céline and Lucette looked the place over. It was furnished in Danish period style, had a well-stocked library and several comfortable bedrooms whose walls were lined with small seascapes by French and Danish painters. So this was how the rich lived in the frozen north? Well, then—not bad!

Petersen left the visitors to unpack. Bébert made himself at home by napping on the silk bedspread in the master bedroom, Lucette went off to explore the garden. Céline spent a quiet afternoon browsing in Mikkelsen's library.

That evening the lawyer himself, just back from Paris, joined them at the dinner table. "No progress in the courts," he told Céline. Obviously unwilling to dwell on the subject of his client's legal case, he'd soon left it far behind. He spoke of books, art, theater and—in response to Lucette's question—the ballet. At that point Céline too began to take an interest. He and his wife inquired in turn about the latest productions and listened attentively to Mikkelsen's long-winded critique of a new Parisian dance company; for once, the talkative attorney had a captive audience.

The dinner table had been positioned to take advantage of the seaward view through large picture windows. They watched a dramatic sunset. On the western horizon a phantasmagoric fleet of galleons was conjured from a single long dark cloud whose billowing sail-like tops soaked up the sun's last gold rays. Mikkelsen told stories about disastrous Baltic storms that had moved in from that direction; the worst of them, several centuries before, had brought about the loss of an entire Swedish fleet.

"In storms along this coast, sailors' lives are often in the hands of the lighthouse keepers. Before the days of the lighthouses, you know, naval signals were transmitted with flags. They had flaghouses all along this coast. There's one still on the property here. Just a hut—we use it as a guest cottage in summer. *Fanehuset,* the local people call it: *house of flags.*" The lawyer paused for effect. "Of course some of the farmers whose families have lived around here for hundreds of years will tell you it means something else—something like *house of the devil*."

"A touch of the Gothic!" Céline's eyes narrowed. "You've been saving that hut for me, no doubt?"

The lawyer ignored his remark. "It's hard to say why they'd call it that." He summoned the caretaker's wife and instructed her to bring in wine.

Dinner was elaborate: a first course of seagull eggs, hard-boiled in their shells, then fish in a sauce of cheese and fresh cream, and breast of wild duck, followed by a chocolate soufflé. The cook's efforts were largely wasted on Céline, who ate sparingly and drank only water.

After three winters in Copenhagen, the brief pastoral idyll of springtime in Mikkelsen's house made Céline feel as if he'd met his angel, no matter what Mik had said about devils' houses! Playing the landed gentleman for once, he occupied himself in the library, writing letters and putting his manuscripts in order, then joined Lucette and Bébert for strolls through fields of wild flowers that bloomed beneath the beech trees.

But his days in the comfort of the main house were numbered. Mikkelsen was expecting other summer guests—most of them prominent, like the attorney general of Denmark and the national poet laureate. Céline and Lucette were abruptly dislodged from Mikkelsen's residence and relegated to Fane-huset, the "guest cottage" by the sea.

Thatch-roofed, freshly daubed with strawberry paint and

bright blue trim on its doors and windows, Fanehuset was quaint enough on first glimpse—like the cottage of some character in an Andersen fairy tale, perhaps. But it lacked basic amenities. Running water, for example. Céline and Lucette had to make their way down a steep path to the Baltic to get seawater for washing, then tote it back up in wooden buckets. For drinking water they had to walk through the woods to Skovly, Mikkelsen's two-story mud-and-plaster "house in the clearing," and use the pump there. The pump at Skovly wasn't always working, however. Sometimes it was necessary to go as far as the neighboring farm for water.

For cooking, Lucette used an ancient peat stove that produced more smoke than heat. It was worst when the fuel wasn't dry. Dry peat was scarce at Klarskovgaard. Deadfall from the beech woods could be burned instead, but accumulating it took hours of foraging and hauling.

Lucette shopped in Korsør for groceries and brought them home on foot or by borrowed bicycle. Céline had been warned by the police to avoid encounters with the local population. When he accompanied Lucette on the hike to Korsør, he waited outside by himself while she went into the shops or the post office to take care of business. Petersen, the caretaker, who went into Korsør by car almost every day, had made it clear from the outset that he didn't consider chauffeuring the foreign visitors to be part of his duties. Céline, for his part, hated asking for favors, particularly if it meant having to feel obliged to someone he disliked. When it happened that Petersen passed the heavily laden couple on the road, he pulled over and waited at the wheel, staring straight ahead until they climbed into the car, then put it into gear and drove on without saying a word. Céline was just as happy not to have to make small talk.

The less he had to do with men the more he liked surrounding himself with other creatures.

At Fanehuset, he and Lucette had quickly established contact with their nonhuman neighbors. She'd begun feeding crumbs to the birds around the cottage. Before long they came in flocks every morning, noisily anticipating her appearance. She talked to them. "You'll soon have these Danish birds chattering in French!" Céline joked.

Bébert took the birds' daily visit as an opportunity to practice his hunting. But it was strictly practice. At best, ten minutes of careful stalking earned him only a glimpse of fleeting wings. One morning when he returned with Lucette from their respective conferences with the birds, it was to find his milk dish surrounded by strange felines. A half-wild stray mother cat had taken advantage of his absence to scavenge a meal for herself and her brood of recently weaned kittens. Well fed himself, Bébert regally disdained the interlopers as they lapped up his breakfast. When they'd finished, the mother cat hurried her kittens away. She brought them back the next day, this time a little more relaxed about her pilfering. Lucette was soon feeding a half-dozen cats.

Céline had adopted Bessy, an Alsatian wolfhound abandoned on the property by a retreating German soldier. Bessy was half wild. Petersen, who'd kept her chained as a result of her fatal attacks on his chickens, called her "a killer" and told Céline that to train her he'd have to use brute force. Céline had seen enough of force. He devised a gentler training method. Tying one end of a rope around his waist, he fastened the other to Bessy's collar. As he sat working at his table in Fanehuset, the big dog was free to circulate in the same area occupied by Bébert and the other cats. Bessy learned in time to tolerate the cats. On cool evenings, they curled up on her back as she lay before the stove.

It was a particularly mild afternoon. Céline sat at a table outside the cabin, writing letters. While he worked, Lucette jumped rope outside Fanehuset, then ran down to the sea for a swim in the always cold waters of the Grand Belt.

After he'd finished his letters, Céline took Bessy along the low rolling cliffs. The tall yellow grass was no impediment to the dog, but it slowed Céline down. He swished the grass blades aside with his walking stick, cleaving a path for himself. Soon he was too tired to walk any farther. He stopped and leaned on the stick, watching the sea. A flock of wild swans glided past. The surface of the Grand Belt glittered with sun reflections. On the deepest waters the sails of fishing boats stood out: rough gray triangles. Céline turned to Bessy. "Look at those sails!" The dog raised her head toward him, alert. "Winding sheets! What else would they fly, navigating past the devil's house!" Bessy let out a howl and loped away, heading down the cliff toward the restless water.

Nothing could have surprised Céline more at this point than a literary visit. A few months after his arrival at Klarskov-gaard, however, a young American professor wrote to him proposing exactly that. After making a name for himself as a "Céline expert" by writing an essay on one of the author's prewar novels, the professor had now decided to follow the aberrant trail of genius all the way back to its source.

Céline, who needed any favorable publicity he could get, accepted the professor's epistolary request for an interview. His first misgivings about what lay ahead didn't arise until he began to receive the young American's preparatory in-quiries. What, the professor asked, was Europe like? Did the continent have indoor plumbing? Hot water? Could meat be found? And was a Russian invasion really imminent?

Reading these letters, Céline realized that having the visitor stay at Fanehuset was out of the question. The fellow had never been away from America before! How was he going to like clambering down a cliff to wash in the ocean? Céline reserved a room in a Korsør hotel.

The appointed day arrived. Céline borrowed Mikkelsen's bicycle and rode in to the Korsør railway station. At the station the young professor, with his horn-rimmed glasses, pale skin and dark curly hair, was easy to spot amid the local cast of pink-cheeked, flaxen-haired Danes. Céline welcomed him with a friendly handshake and words of gratitude, and accompanied him to the hotel. Then, uneasy about the police chief's proscription against "contact with the population" in Korsør, and presuming the visitor would be tired after the long voyage, he excused himself and pedaled back to Klarskovgaard.

The visitor, however, mistook Céline's solicitude for mere bad manners and interpreted his abrupt departure as a calculated insult. The hotel accommodations satisfied him even less. Some of the other guests looked and smelled like bums. Worse, there was a very noisy saloon located directly under his room. He quickly checked out and moved to another hotel—the most expensive one in Korsør; Céline, accustomed to squeezing the most out of every *kroner,* hadn't even considered the place.

The professor was left on his own in a town that bore no resemblance to anything in America. There was no sign of his host for the next two days. The American's distress increased by the hour. When on the third day Céline finally returned to Korsør with Lucette, the professor clearly expected an explanation. Apologies, however, weren't Céline's strong suit. He mumbled something about having stayed away for a few days because he'd been nervous about giving the wrong impression to Korsør police. Seeing him with a foreigner, he said, they might be tempted to think he was plotting an escape to America.

The professor proposed a walk along the small beachfront of Korsør. Céline expressed reluctance, but when he saw that the professor wasn't taking his fears seriously, gave in. All right, perhaps they'd be seen and reported, but it was simply a chance he'd have to take!

The tide was out. They slogged over the brownish-gray sand, the professor in neat gray slacks and fresh white sport shirt and Lucette in crisply laundered floral summer dress making an unlikely pair of companions for the unkempt, seedy Céline—who was stooped and unshaven, his matted hair dangling in strands to the nape of his neck, his broad-sleeved peasant's shirt crumpled and missing several buttons, his baggy pants caked with yellow stains.

Céline's efforts to sustain small talk were defeated by his consciousness of the presence of other people on the beach. Every time they passed someone, he lost track of the professor's conversation and lapsed into restive mutterings. "Those two matrons, see them? Informers! In a hurry to get home and call the police! And that sailor slouching over there—a Communist, for certain!" He turned unhappily to the American. "Do you know how many Cocos there are in Korsør? Six hundred! Just waiting until I make a wrong move, then they'll do me in!"

The professor rented a bicycle for his first trip to Klarskov-gaard. Setting out late one morning, he underestimated the midday heat and the difficulty of the five-mile trek over bad roads. By the time he reached the winding path that led to Fanehuset, he was sweat-soaked and trundling the bicycle by hand. A sudden vision stopped him in his tracks: out in front of the thatched cabin, a naked woman! Her dark hair tied back into a turban, svelte and muscular, she had the serene, blank-eyed self-absorption of a Picasso acrobat. She obviously hadn't noticed him and went on doing perfect pliés and arabesques on a mat in the sun. The professor stood open-mouthed, grasping his handlebars. Just then Lucette looked up. She smiled at him. The professor blushed deeply, stammering out an embarrassed greeting. Amused by his confusion, Lucette was laughing as she disappeared into the cottage. A moment later Céline—fully if sloppily clothed—hobbled out to receive his guest.

In the cramped parlor of the cottage, Lucette, now wrapped in an oriental robe, served tea for the men. Céline pointed to the banged-up metal teapot in her hands. "You see that pot? It went through the flames of Germany with us!"

The professor looked ill at ease as he pulled out a notebook. Would his host mind answering a few questions? Céline shrugged. The professor launched into his interview. At first the questioning was purely literary, much as Céline had expected. Then the interrogator changed his tone and said abruptly, "I'm a Jew, you know."

"So I assumed," said Céline.

"It doesn't bother you?"

"No."

"Then would you mind my asking some questions about your attitude toward the Jews?"

Céline couldn't conceal his annoyance. "So you've come thousands of miles just to play the role of prosecutor?"

"Not at all. But people are entitled to know."

Céline threw back his head. "I don't exist anymore; I'm dead; I belong to history."

"Hitler also claimed to belong to history. One can't wash away crimes in a few expressions of Olympian fatalism."

Céline had heard enough. Rising to his feet, he sent curses ricocheting around the low-beamed ceiling of Fanehuset.

"You want to know about Hitler? Fine! Hitler—a true shit-brain, if there ever was one! Hitler never had a real revolutionary program. Just schemes for killing people! He should have given up back in '40, when he had the chance! The thing was all over by then, wasn't it? Instead, what did Hitler do? Dragged the slaughter out for half a decade. Made the whole world suffer for his idiocy! What a disastrous little ball of shit!"

The professor nodded attentively, jotting notes. "I've been re-reading *L'École des cadavres*," he said. "Weren't you saying there that you approved of what Hitler was doing about the Jews?"

Céline turned white. So he had a Grand Inquisitor on his hands! "The answer to this burning question is simple. I never had *any idea* what Hitler was planning for the Jews! No idea at all!" He sputtered, the sides of his mouth leaking saliva. "Ask anybody who knows me! I never said a word in favor of injuring a single Jew. I have nothing against Jews! I had one complaint against them: They're so much smarter than the Aryans! I saw that the Aryans simply couldn't compete with them! That's the sort of thing that causes wars, the imbalance of economic power! And Europe was in bad shape at that time. One solution would have been to transport the

Jews to Palestine. I may have mentioned that—all right! But that wasn't the same thing as advocating persecution. 'Relocate them' didn't mean 'kill them,' after all!''

Lucette, made nervous by this kind of talk, poured Céline some more tea and, as she bent over the cup, whispered to him to watch what he was saying—after all, he hardly knew the American. But it was too late; Céline had passed beyond caution. Concentrating his attention on the visitor, he waved her away impatiently.

"I've answered all these questions a hundred times before, from Vestre Faengsel to the North Pole! I have to repeat myself over and over, but no one ever seems to listen. Always the same thing! The Jews this and the Jews that! Even my own lawyer—acting like a good liberal missionary, forever praising all the prominent Jews he knows. All for my benefit, as if I were a savage to be converted!''

"You can hardly blame him. . . ." The professor looked down, astounded that Céline should be so insensitive as to say such things to him. "The pamphlets you wrote before the war *did*—after all—contribute to . . ." He hesitated, searching for the courage to say what was in his heart. "I mean, your books must have had *some* effect on what happened later."

Céline exploded: "I never hurt the Jews! I had nothing against them! It was the other way around. They had it in for *me*! Don't ask me why! Look at the way they fucked me around at the League of Nations, the way they squeezed me out of my clinic at Clichy! I saw how they operate, that time! Oh, that was classic. Working quarter, a dozen comrades in the town hall—and then every time there's a vacancy they bring in another Jew from the East! Pretty soon the place is practically oriental! And why?" Céline concluded triumphantly: "Orders from Moscow!"

The agitated professor set down his notebook. "Come, now, surely that's an unfair generalization. All Jews aren't alike—and all Jews aren't Communists." He removed his glasses, making him look even younger, and pointed them accusatively at Céline. "You're always jumping to conclusions!"

"I jump only from my own experience. Something you're disqualified from understanding!"

There was a heavy, hostile silence. Lucette began clearing away the plates and cups. Céline stared at the American.

"And how are things at the hotel? Civilized enough to suit you this time, I hope?"

"Fine, thank you." The visitor's tone was stiff and formal.

"Not too noisy for sleeping?" Céline's solicitous smile carried a faint satiric twist.

"No."

"Sleeping's not easy this time of year for anyone around here. The mosquitos are bad enough to make one long for winter. Isn't that right, Luci? Though they say the winters are even worse!"

"Louis is tired today," Lucette put in.

They all sat quietly.

"It's the undertow turning." Céline was facing the window, with a faraway look in his eyes. "Don't you hear it?"

They listened to the rumbling noise made by the Baltic as

it surged up on the beach a few hundred yards away. The professor, who appeared baffled by Céline's remark about the undertow, turned to Lucette for a sign.

"I hear the sea, that's all," she said.

Her husband still stared toward the seaward window. "No, there's something else." He listened. "When the undertow takes over, pulling the water back out . . . I hear it often at night. You mean you've never noticed it?"

The professor stayed another week in Korsør, but after the "interview" at Klarskovgaard Céline began to heed Lucette's warnings about being more circumspect. He grew cautious not only about what he said in the professor's presence, but also—since he now sensed his personal life was under observation along with his work and ideas—about how he behaved. On his next trip to town, he wore clean trousers, sported a fresh haircut (the handiwork of Lucette) and conducted himself with exaggerated formality. The professor immediately noticed the change and took it as a sign he'd pressed too far with his questions. Thereafter the two men tiptoed around each other, neither willing to risk another serious confrontation.

They saw each other for the last time in Korsør on the eve of the American's departure. It was a glum meeting on an afternoon that resembled Céline's mood—dark and cloudy. His somber parting statement to his visitor was "that's life"— uttered with a sigh that seemed to acknowledge the unbridgeable distance between them as merely another of the hard facts of existence. The professor laughed nervously, evidently regarding the remark as banal—yet another instance of the sad condition into which the once-great writer had descended.

In September, after the last of Mikkelsen's summer guests had departed, Céline and Lucette moved into Skovly, the two-story mud-and-thatch "house in a clearing" at the far edge of the lawyer's property. There they would get their first taste of winter in the wilds of the North.

And winter wasn't slow in coming.

There were trees around Skovly, a beech forest that was already losing its leaves when Céline moved in. At first he walked there with Bessy in the afternoons, but as the days grew short, the trees seemed to gather up a stillness of menacing dimensions—and to unleash it on his wary head whenever he ventured under them. He found himself staying away from the forest, depressed by its brooding silences. Better the wind and noise of the open coast!

Gales blew for days on end, churning the waters of the Grand Belt into a fine mesh of restless whitecaps. Farther out to sea the surface leveled off and moved in large swelling planes that changed with distance from a flat olive drab to an iridescent gray-green—the color of the trunks of the now nearly leafless beeches behind Skovly.

For ten days in October the sun didn't appear, then late one afternoon, when Céline was out walking with Bessy, it emerged through long bluish clouds above the horizon and blazed forth a cascade of yellow light that lasted only a few minutes before the clouds again closed over.

The brief apparition had its effect on Céline, who was always on the alert for signs. But Bessy seemed uninterested, her attention diverted by gulls and curlews that mewed into the wind, straining to make progress as they headed out to sea to fish.

With the dog waiting obediently at his side, Céline stood looking out toward the spot where the sun had vanished. Every so often he said something, but Bessy paid no attention, and his words were lost in the wind. He didn't bother to make sentences: "the pull . . . the cut . . . the drag . . . the fall!" His black cape and white scarf billowed out around him, signal flags marking his claim to this barren nub of terrain at the end of the world.

A wet, sodden spell at the beginning of November ushered in high winds and low temperatures that bespoke asperities to come. The pump failed at Skovly. To get water Céline had to plod through freezing winds with a wheelbarrow and a ten-liter metal drum (leftover of a German tank crew) to the farmer's house. It was a forty-five-minute trip. The gusts knifing off the Baltic snapped the ends of his scarf back against his face with enough force to sting tears into his eyes. He plowed on, his mind drifting back to the days when he'd toted fifty-pound jewelry cases all over Paris as a delivery boy. Forty-five years gone by, and he was still a beast of burden! Life was like that! You tried to pull yourself up, but something was always sucking you back down! Gravity, death, it was all the same: a force that was constantly dragging you back, a kind of undertow . . . pulling you down. . . .

December: The mercury kept dropping. If Céline left water in the drum outside the house overnight, in the morning it was frozen solid.

Living things handled the cold in one of two ways—either by defense or by flight. Lucette's birds had long since taken the latter course, disappearing southward to be replaced on the pine branches by tiny prismatic jewels of frost. But the domestic animals of Skovly couldn't flee; they grew long, thick protective coats and huddled together in a heap at night; the humans took note, and imitated as best they could.

Mikkelsen had gone to France for the winter; only the caretaker and his family remained on the estate. Céline and Lucette rarely saw them. The nights continued to expand, getting longer and deeper.

One night a heavy nocturnal snowfall took the couple by surprise. Céline woke up to a lifeless world. He cried out to Lucette from the window: "Buried alive!" The front door refused to budge. They had to wait until late afternoon for Petersen to get around to digging them out.

For half an hour the caretaker's shovel strokes slowly approached. Then finally the door burst open, and he stood frowning and panting before them, the snow-dusted fur lining of his parka hood making a dazzling halo around his red cheeks.

"Brought back from the dead, like Lazarus!" Céline stepped forward to offer a grateful handshake.

Petersen, a strict churchgoing Lutheran, recoiled stiffly. "You may blaspheme all you like in those books of yours," he said, "but please don't do it around me!" Shouldering his shovel like a field weapon, he glared at Céline, wheeled and trudged off up the freshly dug path through the snow.

While Mikkelsen was away, Petersen and his wife looked after the vacant main house. On days when the caretaker was in Korsør on business, Céline sometimes slipped into the unheated house and spent an hour or two in the library with a blanket and a book.

One dark afternoon when thick snow flurries scattered against the library windows like pillow stuffing blown in off the Grand Belt, he sat idly leafing through the single book of Mikkelsen's he most prized: a well-worn vintage edition of the *Grande Encyclopédie Française*. Turning its pages at random, he immersed himself in the measured prose of a pre-1914 world which he preferred to the present one—and which was no less removed in spirit from it than life on another planet might have been.

His eye fell on an illustration. It was a photo of the statues of Gog and Magog at the Guildhall in London. Even before looking at the accompanying text, he was struck by something repulsive and fascinating in the figures' gleefully mischievous faces. What was it that seemed so recognizable there?

Of course, who could miss it? The prophet of *Revelations*

had been correct: Evil was loose in the world; it was dropping through the ages like a plummet that hadn't yet touched bottom, and every so often you noticed its passage in the twisted, grinning faces of those whose souls it grazed as it fell!

"Anybody who comes to this godforsaken place expecting something out of the movies romantic exile, comfortable smoking rooms and exalted outlaws—will be in for an unpleasant surprise," Céline wrote to a friend in Paris who was considering a visit. "It's a superglacial cloister, the vault at the end of the world where death and night are kept."

Sitting in his frigid cloister, a yellowed newspaper photo of the old mill in Montmartre—the view from his former rue Lepic apartment—tacked on the mildewed plaster wall in front of him, a rug on his lap and heated bricks beneath his feet, he continued to struggle with the novel he'd begun in prison. He tried to block out his surroundings, but their impact on his senses was too immediate—the air, for instance, thick with smells of peat smoke, wet fur, melting candle wax and leeks being cooked. In the silence of the room, the sounds of his sentences drifted away before he could catch them.

Outside, it was a dead world. The Baltic ruled everything, even the bone-white sky which merged imperceptibly into the mist-sheeted outer waters like a slab of blank marble sliding into soapy dishwater. Nothing moved. Skovly's walls wore a thick hair shirt of frost and mildew.

As late as April, wind still shook the roof at night, but

finally the mornings began to carry new sounds: In place of the roaring winds, one heard the crackling, creeping, trickling noises of life seeping back into the landscape. Small animals began to move around in the beech trees behind Skovly, and a few wild flowers popped up between the planks of Lucette's makeshift exercise platform out in front—their pale watery colors looking fragile and temporary against the dense black-green backdrop of the still slumbering pine forest.

In May the prevailing winds turned. A soft breeze came in warm and fresh from the south. Céline took Bessy and walked the beech woods for the first time since fall. There were so many birds that the big dog barely had time to recover from one crashing pursuit before the next began. Overhead, returning storks wheeled across the sky, headed inland to find nesting spots after wintering in Algeria or Tunisia.

The forest floor had erupted with tiny starlike flowers, each one as shiny white as pure candle wax, growing in banks as soft and thick underfoot as a spongy new carpet. These banks of anemones reflected their collective luminosity back up into the lime-green aerial translucencies of the beeches, whose first leaves had just begun to fill out the canopy of branches overhead.

Bessy bounded forward, plunging through thick underbrush. Trying to keep up, Céline moved faster, tromping over flowers, pulling himself along on his walking stick. His heart beat hard against his chest. The dog splashed into a pool of stagnant water and came out shaking off water drops in a propulsive shower. She stood across the pool from her master, panting and eager to continue the fun.

He stopped and gestured. The dog looked back at him doubtfully for a moment. Then there was a quick covert movement from a few yards deeper in the woods. Twigs snapped; the white tail of a startled rabbit appeared as it exploded into flight. Bessy charged off into the woods on the track of the fleeing animal.

Like the migratory storks, Mikkelsen returned to Klarskov-gaard every spring. This spring, though, he came back with a bad conscience.

Wary of Céline's grand rages, the lawyer had long since fallen into the habit of tailoring the truth in ways calculated to skirt them. When discussing delicate subjects with his client and houseguest, he was always careful to censor out anything that might be likely to trigger Céline's temper. And this time his secret was particularly onerous. Something had befallen him on his recent trip to France. . . .

Though he'd promised Céline he'd exchange the gold only in small increments, the increasing difficulty of making piece-meal exchanges had finally caused the lawyer to suspend the agreed-upon precautions. On this latest trip he'd carried along with him the entire remaining stock of gold pieces. Dealing with Céline's money had become a tedious chore; he'd looked forward to having it over with once and for all.

But carrying gold through the partitioned state of Germany was always risky. There were unexpected border searches.

It was the lawyer's bad luck to have run into one. He'd gone south by car ferry as usual, then driven across the frontier at Flensburg, and was about to enter the British sector when he was halted for a customs inspection. A British soldier had lifted open the trunk of his car, turned over a pile of blankets, found Céline's gold wrapped inside and confiscated it. Only Mikkelsen's record with the Danish Resistance had saved him from being arrested. The gold was now in the hands of the British army, officially classified as contraband.

Céline had to be told. The lawyer came back to Klarskov-gaard intending to tell him. But when the time came, on the evening of their first dinner together, after the usual polite talk, he lost his nerve and couldn't bring himself to speak up. When Céline asked what was bothering him, he replied that he was distracted by business worries. Céline was left in the dark.

7.
THE WAIT

Time passed: not the constructive kind of time that weaves together into an organic pattern all the complicated strands of a life, but the special deconstructive time of exile, which works the opposite way, slowly unraveling you from the inside.

You had to wait; but waiting itself had a way of making things worse. "From the minute we start expecting some end to all this," Céline told Lucette, "we're already dead."

Life on Mikkelsen's estate went along as usual. The lawyer and his big-shot friends, the caretaker and his family, they all had their personal histories and motives and plans to occupy them—their lives building up in a steady progression from the past into the future. That continuity was what gave their lives meaning. For Céline, however, shunted once again off to Fanehuset to make room for the annual influx of summer guests, there was no longer any sense of progression in events at all, no continuity except the bad continuity of a B-movie.

Watching the others go about their lives, he felt an odd detachment in time, as if the daily existence of Klarskovgaard was a scene frozen in the past: The people were figures in a natural history museum diorama, and himself an observer viewing them through the glass of a display case.

It occurred to Céline that the physicists' theory of relativity had a personal application for him. In his exile, time had become a distorting medium, letting the past seep through into the present and turning the present into a hallucination.

He went to bed at seven every night, but slept little.

There were evenings when he simply lay with his eyes open, training his attention on the sound of the waves hitting the shore below the cottage. Sometimes in the middle of the warmest nights a breeze picked up. Inaudible because of the sea noise, it could be noticed only by the sudden odor of pines with which it filled Fanehuset. Then perhaps a horse would cry out, somewhere off in the night. That was the caretaker's horse, an old mare Petersen used for hauling. The sound was as desolate as a lost child's wail. Echoing in the whinny of the disturbed mare was another, older noise—the cries of men and horses dying in battle. The first night his regiment had moved into combat position: a scent of pines on the air there, too. In the distance, heavy guns made a noise that came up through your shoes . . . no, it was only the rumbling of the Baltic.

He reached out to the bedside table, fumbled for the veronal.

The breeze stirred again. Those pines . . . he drifted back. Another night in Flanders, a different field, pines at one end of it. He'd been riding toward them, breakneck—a volunteer mission, carrying a message, the recklessness of youth! Suddenly the night had lit up. Not the midnight sun, as here in Denmark, but death putting on a show for him. What fireworks! And then . . . the red mud. Face down in it, among dead men. He'd been the only one to survive. To stay alive! And for what? To come to this . . .

An owl called out of the trees beyond Skovly, and the night breeze carried the sound all the way down to the summer cottage where he lay listening.

Céline was called
to appear for a hearing on his case at the Place Vendôme in
Paris on December 15, 1949. From Klarskovgaard he wrote
to inform the presiding judge that physical disabilities pre-
vented him from appearing at the hearing. His health, he
said, had been destroyed by a ten-year-long defamation cam-
paign. He could scarcely rise from bed. How could he appear
in such a state?

Writing to the judge gave Céline occasion to challenge the
motives of the Courts of Justice. Did the court really want
justice, he asked, or was it merely seeking "to skin the cat?"
"I know what's expected," he told the judge. "I'm supposed

to play the sacrificial victim in an iron-curtain comedy. All right, then! Let them have it their way. I turned over the keys to the port of Calais! I was Hitler's mistress!"

The day of the hearing dawned cold and gray at Klarskov-gaard. By late morning a light snowfall had begun. The dead grass stalks that rose out of the yellow soil of uncultivated fields at the edge of the estate slowly turned white in the wind that battered off the Baltic.

Bundled up against the weather, Céline went at midday to the caretaker's.

Petersen was cutting wood out in front of the house. He wore only a light windbreaker, but the work had brought high color to his cheeks. Resting on the long ax between strokes, he watched Céline slowly make his way up the path.

"The boss called last night. Said your trial's today—and that you won't be there."

Céline shivered and turned to face out of the wind. "And he's not there either."

Petersen spat on the frozen ground. "He's got business in Copenhagen." He lifted his ax to head level, examined the blade with narrowed eyes, then let it slide down and began stroking the long handle. "You're not his only client, you know."

Céline glanced toward the house. "I'd like to use the phone," he said, conciliatory.

The caretaker placed a log on the block for splitting. He

raised the ax into the air, where it hung poised for a moment, then brought it down in a long violent stroke. The blade slammed into the log, sinking in several inches.

"Leave the money in the usual place," he said.

Céline's phone call was a short one. When it was over he made his way back to Skovly. The snow was heavier now. It tufted his eyelids, glazed the gray stubble on his cheeks, crusted his cape with a fine down. Flakes swirled into his mouth, melted on his tongue.

Lucette threw a woolen blanket over him when he came in. "You talked to Naud?"

He nodded, teeth chattering, and pulled the blanket around himself. "It went as expected."

"So there's mercy, after all!"

"Mercy?" His laugh was caustic.

"But a postponement, then?"

"A 'remission,' Naud calls it. You know these lawyers. They have their own ballet! *Entrechats, pliés, sine die, dies irae* . . . "

Lucette frowned. "What does it mean?"

"More delays and fiddling!"

"Did Naud say anything else?"

"He says none of the jurors has read my books—except one, a woman."

"That's good, isn't it? The women, they always like you."

"Evidently this one's a proper bourgeois. One of those businessmen's wives who like to keep up with 'culture.' She looked into the *Journey*, it seems. Found it vulgar!"

Lucette laughed.

Céline noticed the pool of water shed by the melting snow on his boots. He began tugging them off.

A new hearing date was set: February 21, 1950. Céline instructed Mikkelsen to forward to Naud a doctor's letter as "proof" that he was too ill to attend his own trial.

The week before the trial, *Cahiers de la Resistance*, the official journalistic organ of the Action Committee of the French Resistance, published a special "Céline issue." In it, the exiled writer was treated as a subhuman monster, a figure so deplorable that history couldn't supply comparable examples.

More articles followed daily from the left-wing press. On the trial day itself *l'Humanité* loaded all the hatred of a decade into a final editorial as subtle as a firing squad. So Céline was at last to be judged? Excellent, said the Communist journal. "Let justice strike with the greatest rigor."

The dark, wood-paneled courtroom at the Place Vendôme was packed. The atmosphere in the room was something between that of a funeral and that of a public hanging. Rubberneckers made up a good part of the crowd; at several points their whispered commentary on the proceedings drew reproving stares from the judge. But there was another group of courtroom spectators who sat gravely, obviously in some personal apprehension as to the outcome; these people had once been friends or acquaintances of the defendant.

The prosecutor, René Charasse, urbane and distinguished-looking in his black robes, informed the jurors that the absent defendant was on trial for wartime writings of his that might have aided the enemy. He named the pamphlet *Les Beaux Draps*, printed in 1941, and also several interviews and letters to the editor published in right-wing papers. When the names of these papers were read, there were nods and murmurs around the courtroom. Charasse calmly went on, adding that the defendant was being held accountable for membership in the pro-German organization, the European Circle, and for making two trips into enemy territory—in 1942 and again in 1944.

Charasse then talked for a few minutes about the defendant's character. Céline, he said, was a natural loner. He was intrinsically incapable of collaboration with anyone, at any time, for any reason. Several flamboyant, self-justifying letters he'd received from Céline before the trial had convinced Charasse of one thing in particular, he said: that their author was mentally imbalanced. In view of this, Charasse told the court, he regretted that it hadn't been possible to have Céline examined by psychiatrists.

As to sentencing, Charasse concluded, he had determined that there was insufficient evidence to apply the treason statute, article seventy-five, to the case at hand. In his view Céline's deeds warranted punishment, but only as prescribed by the less stringent article eighty-three, governing "acts detrimental to national security." Accordingly, Charasse said—and here he turned to the judge—he recommended a light sentence.

With Céline absent, his lawyers could not argue his case. When Charasse sat down, they remained at their desks as the judge had a clerk read out their documentary evidence: some character testimonials contributed by others, and then Céline's own statements of defense, the first written in November 1946 at Vestre Faengsel, the second composed at Skovly a few weeks before the trial.

This new statement answered Charasse's charges point by point. Céline declared that when he'd written *Les Beaux Draps*, he'd known *nothing* about the deportation of Jews. That particular pamphlet was a work of *patriotism*, directed against opportunistic "neo-collaborators." And as for any letters of his that might have found their way into collaborationist papers, those were either counterfeits, or else private correspondence published without his knowledge or consent. What could he do about that? As for the European Circle, they'd listed him as a member without his permission. He'd gone to some trouble to have his name taken off their membership rolls. And the trips to Germany, those weren't acts of "collaboration" either. The one in 1942 had been a pretext for meeting Karen Jensen, while his northward flight two years later had been motivated not by political ideology, but by a simple desire to save his neck: "I'd received, for the past three years, over the radio and in the daily papers, at least three death threats per day." The clerk read all this out loud from the documents before him, while members of the jury took notes.

Then, at the instruction of the prosecutor, the clerk shuffled through more papers and began to read from the allegedly "guilty" passages of *Les Beaux Draps*.

Up to this point, those who'd known Céline personally had been as stiffly silent as a Calvinist congregation listening to a lecture on original sin. But the clerk's flat monotone couldn't entirely suppress the insane black humor of Céline's writing. Faces began to turn red. As the reading continued, a woman in the back row stifled a giggle. Ripples of laughter were soon spreading through the courtroom. "If Céline is guilty," the spectators seemed to be saying despite themselves, "so are we."

The six jurors, five men and one woman, listened and looked on in great perplexity. Could such a concoction of comedy and hysteria ever have been taken seriously by anyone?

They did not take long to bring a verdict.

It was already twilight in Seeland. Out the windows the bare beech trunks hulked under a mosslike webbing of ice, huge bluish-gray piers of some eternal bridge of sighs. The stringy slate-colored clouds that trailed out toward the Grand Belt were lit with an eerie pink underglow.

Before a struggling peat fire that issued more smoke than

heat into the room, Céline stood talking with his wife. He was just back from making another call to France.

"After all this, Luci, they've settled for cutting my head off halfway! A year in the hole, fifty thousand in fines and half of whatever I earn the rest of my working days—that's what our generous countrymen have in store for me!"

His face was white, his voice low and cold. "And the denouement . . . 'condemned to a state of national disgrace.' Think of that! Unworthy to live!"

"You *can't* go to prison again," Lucette said firmly. "Not after what happened in the other place."

He walked over to the windows and looked out into the dark beech woods. "Not to prison," he said. "Not after Vestre, never." He turned back to her. "The time in Vestre seems to be the half of my neck they've left me, though. They say the law doesn't make you pay twice for one crime. So if the lawyers can arrange credit for the time in Vestre—"

He paused, seeing the hope rise in her face. "No point getting ahead of ourselves." He shrugged. " 'All things in due time,' says Naud."

They stayed up together to talk. A cold fog rolled in off the water and pressed itself against the ice-covered windows. "White nights!" Céline paced in front of the fire. "How many of them we've been through, Luci!"

But nothing could be solved by talking, when so much

remained in doubt. Just before dawn Lucette went off to bed. Céline, too restless to sleep, went outside with Bessy.

The fog bank had begun to drift back out toward the Baltic. The sky was pearly gray, still hung with stars. Man and dog moved along, lost in separate worlds. They went through a stand of pines. The sun came up like a brass lemon shining weakly through the pine branches, lighting up the forest enough to make it clear that frost was everywhere, clinging to the bluish-green boughs, glazing the needles underfoot.

There was a sudden motion. A dark spot moved against the white ground—a vole fleeing the intruders, making a dash for the cover of a thin bank of snow. Bessy snapped to attention, poised to spring, but the vole ducked into the snow-bank just in time. Bessy sniffed with interest at the bank. Then Céline said something to her. She relaxed and gave up the pursuit.

"Papers, papers!" Céline ranted to Lucette. "Birth, death, marriage, prison, there's no difference!"

His fate now hung on the lawyers' motion of "equivalence." Would the French court accept his time in Vestre Faengsel as a suitable equivalent of the one-year jail term in his sentence? Did the two punishments cover the same offense? A ruling on this point would come only after all the appropriate papers had been filed.

"Nothing in the world can take place without endless papers!" He pushed himself away from his desk, flinging several loose sheets into the air. They resettled slowly to the floor.

"And if the paperwork stretches from here to the moon and fills up all its craters, still no business can get done, because all the lawyers and judges are off swilling or snoring!"

A cold blast from the north hit Klarskovgaard at the end of March, bringing with it more ice and snow—and a half-frozen lady journalist from the Paris magazine *Radar*, who managed to make her way through the storm to Skovly, only to find a glum Céline laid up in bed, sick and reluctant to talk. The reporter went home and told her Parisian readers that "Céline, the swashbuckler, 'big-mouth' Céline" was dead and gone—replaced by "a poor broken devil." His picture, reproduced next to one of Ingrid Bergman inside the glossy magazine, showed a figure more to be pitied than excoriated. He looked ashen, dazed and exhausted, supporting the reporter's contention that the "Monster of Montmartre" was no longer worth attacking.

A French arrest warrant still dangled over Céline's head. Naud told him they'd reached a legal impasse. In order to settle the "equivalence" matter, Céline would have to appear *in person* in a French court. Naud suggested that he comply.

Céline said no. His attorneys could assure him as much as they liked. It wasn't *they* who'd be exposing themselves to a visit to the penitentiary at Fresnes! No, he wasn't going!

The prospect of a return to France, so real only a few months before, began to fade. Through the long muggy sum-

mer at Fanehuset Céline sat staring at the unfinished manuscript before him on his desk, now and then writing a line
or two, leaning his head on his hand and daydreaming about
impossible escapes to places he'd never been—to Chile, to
Canada, to Corsica.

Pure fantasy. Without papers, there wasn't a single border
he could safely cross!

That fall Naud went off to Canada, leaving Céline to deal
with a new legal problem. The French court was taking steps
to enforce the part of his sentence that stipulated the confis-
cation of half his property. In danger of being confiscated
were large sums in unpaid royalties for his prewar books and
back payments from his World War I military pension, which
had been stacking up in France throughout his exile. The
prospective loss of these assets, earned at the cost of so much
pain, enraged Céline. He complained to Lucette that he was
being stripped of his skin by madmen.

It was Céline's sixth bleak Christmas in Denmark, his seventh
in exile. On the feast of Advent a high wall of black cloud
massed over the Grand Belt. It started to rain. The rain kept
on for days, soaking the caretaker's crèche at Klarskovgaard.
The straw turned rotten. Skovly's interior walls erupted in
patches of fine green mold. "Perfect weather for rheuma-
tism," Céline grumbled. In Korsør the talk was of Eisen-
hower's visit to Copenhagen. The American "hero" had been

hooted at by Danish Communists. There were anti-American demonstrations staged by the dockworkers. Céline shielded his own opinions under an umbrella of silence. He stayed away from Korsør. Politics was like the rain; unless you took shelter, it came down on your head.

Fate was a wayward and unpredictable mechanism that towered over human beings: Its workings took place in the dark, you were tossed around like a flea in a squall, there was nothing you could do and only silence lay beyond.

A January snowstorm blew in off the Grand Belt and blanketed Klarskovgaard with a foot of soft white powder whose depths, when stepped into, briefly turned an icy blue. For that moment, while one looked down, the inside of the snowbank emanated an unearthly aura—as if one had stumbled through the planet's crust into a cold world of sapphires and liquid ether.

It continued to snow. Through the windows of Skovly the

blizzard was a gray vortex. Luminous silver swirls were suspended in it like frozen catherine's wheels. Céline watched
the snow from beneath a pile of animals and blankets. Vertigo
had driven him to bed. A wooden board across his lap held
several loose white pages. Every few minutes he looked down
and wrote a line. "What frigid fireworks! An orgy of glacial
tornadoes!"

Several days of rain followed the snowstorm. Everything
melted, turned brown and sodden, then refroze. When Céline
was well enough to get out of bed, it was only to find that
the pump at Skovly had broken down. He tried to haul the
water drum to the farmer's. On the way, his right arm went
numb. He felt shooting pains in his head and chest. Moments
later, he found himself lying in a ditch beside the road. Abandoning his barrow and drum, he slowly retraced his steps to
Skovly. There Lucette forced him back into bed.

That night he had an unusual dream. His soul—himself—
had somehow become disembodied; it was now yoked to a
separate being, a huge, friendly and radiant angel. This angel,
who spoke the demotic French of the Montmartre cafés and
had a way of winking at him as though they were partners
in some benign conspiracy, took his hand and led him along
the road to Korsør. The road was in a bad state, muddy and
icy at the same time; here and there they passed mired vehicles. Inside one of the stalled automobiles—a German staff
car—he saw Fernand de Brinon, gesticulating angrily behind
frosted glass windows. The chauffeur of the car was Boemelburg, who wore a malicious smile.

Then the angel led him past the stalled cars, showing him

where the muddy road had congealed into a gleaming crystal pathway. Soon Korsør loomed ahead. It had become a bright city with high glass towers. They hurried along, hand in hand. Just as they were about to enter the city, the road crossed a narrow bridge. Below, Céline made out a terrifying abyss: it gaped down into a blackness that issued from the center of the earth. Fumes rose from it, the ghastly smells of burning phosphorus and incinerated flesh. From miles below, a sound of explosions drifted up. In the dream Céline felt he was going to faint. He reached out to grasp the hand of the angel. But as he turned, he saw that the angel was moving toward him in a strange way. The angel was entering into him; they had merged and become one. Now Céline was alone, midway across this bridge that got narrower with every step he took. The bridge swayed. He grabbed for the handrail, but there was none.

In February 1951, the files of collaborators still under the jurisdiction of the Courts of Justice were turned over to a French military tribunal for final disposition. One of these cases was Céline's.

His defense was now in the hands not of Albert Naud, who'd had little success, but of a second attorney, Jean-Louis Tixier-Vignancour. Tixier-Vignancour, as well known in right-wing circles as Naud, but a much more low-keyed courtroom figure, had been working in a subordinate role as part of Céline's defense team. He stepped forward at this point to take over the case.

The first barrier between Céline and freedom was the French arrest warrant. In March Tixier-Vignancour filed a petition before the military tribunal. In it he described the shaky health of his client, whom he identified only by the name Ferdinand Destouches.

This Destouches was willing to appear for a hearing on his case, the lawyer maintained; but, being very sick, the fellow didn't believe he'd survive imprisonment and was therefore unwilling to risk exposure to arrest. Accepting the lawyer's guarantee that defendant Destouches would present himself in court, the tribunal agreed to remove the long-standing warrant. Tixier-Vignancour was instructed to have this Destouches on hand for a hearing to take place a month later.

The lawyer flew to Denmark. He managed to convince a Korsør taxi driver to negotiate the muddy track to Klarskovgaard in the middle of a rainstorm. The driver approached only as far as the turnoff at the edge of the estate, where the dirt road turned into a morass, and dropped him off there. Tixier-Vignancour, in an elegant business suit and carrying a briefcase full of legal papers, had to wade across a bog to get to his client's door. Minutes later he sat with steaming socks in front of Skovly's smoky peat fire, outlining his strategy to Céline.

"Frankly," he said, "the judges of the tribunal are no different in most respects from the average French soldier. To them, the name 'Ferdinand Destouches' will mean nothing. Another small-time collaborator, that's all." He paused, his eyes twinkling in the firelight. "We might describe their state as blissful ignorance. We will try to help them remain in that state. No testimonials, no pronouncements, just silence."

Céline understood. He smiled at the humor of it.

"So we're in agreement?"

"Yes," Céline said. "From this moment Louis-Ferdinand Céline is dead and buried."

"The next step is a feint," said the lawyer. "You will take part."

He snapped open his briefcase and pulled out a sheaf of papers—a passport application. He handed the papers to Céline, who looked them over and then, with a flourish, signed them "Ferdinand Destouches."

Tixier-Vignancour took the application to the French embassy in Copenhagen. There, an obliging embassy official— well aware that "Destouches" was in fact the "Céline" whose name was at the top of the list of local expatriates to be denied travel permits—supplied the lawyer with a letter stating it was impossible for the man in question to obtain either a passport or a visa. With this letter in his briefcase, Tixier-Vignancour returned to France.

Back in Paris, he presented the embassy letter to the military tribunal. The rejected passport application was accepted by the tribunal as pro forma proof of Céline's inability to appear in court. A hearing on the case—to be held in absentia—was set for April 20.

Now Tixier-Vignancour filed another petition with the

tribunal. He requested that the Destouches case be reconsidered in light of a somewhat obscure 1947 statute. The statute provided for grants of amnesty to collaborators who'd been convicted to prison sentences of no longer than three years, and who'd also suffered disabling war injuries. Defendant Destouches, the lawyer pointed out in his petition, had been disabled in 1914, and was now facing a one-year sentence. Therefore, Tixier-Vignancour contended, Ferdinand Destouches was eligible for amnesty under the 1947 statute.

This time the hearing date approached with no advance fanfare in the newspapers. Tixier-Vignancour deliberately neglected to inform not only the press, but even his fellow attorney, Naud. Céline himself, following the lawyer's instructions, kept the hearing a secret from the same friends and supporters who'd provided testimonials and jammed the courtroom seats a year earlier.

The product of these precautions was a largely empty hearing chamber on the morning of April 20. Only the clerks, military judges and Tixier-Vignancour were present. The judges restricted themselves to consideration of the documentary evidence presented by Tixier-Vignancour. The 1947 statute was discussed. Its terms were clear, as was the eligibility of the defendant. The name "Destouches" rang no bells, even for the president of the tribunal (who was later to explain, "In literature I stopped at Flaubert!"). The proceedings were simple and straightforward, much to the relief of the judges, who'd had their fill of complicated collaboration cases that dragged on for weeks and even months. For once, none of them was late for his lunch.

To Céline, the night before the hearing seemed interminable. There was no dreaming of angels now! Deep in the night Lucette was awakened by the sound of his voice. He was sitting up in bed talking out loud to himself. *"Merde!* What an ass I've been! Stubborn! Pigheaded! A mule! All for knowledge that's worth nothing!"

At dawn he got up, gulped aspirin, shuffled to his desk. The piles of handwritten manuscript pages stared up at him. He sat down and absently began to reconstruct a sentence he'd written the day before. He tried several different approaches, tinkering until things fell into place and the sentence did what he wanted it to. He sighed and went on to the next one. A few thousand more of these, and perhaps he'd have a novel some day!

He was still writing at midmorning, when one of Petersen's sons appeared at the door to inform him that there was a phone call from France.

He put his pen aside and followed the boy on the path across the estate. Mikkelsen's apple trees were in blossom, a snowy sea of white. In the sun the air was warm. Buttery light suffused the woods beyond the orchard. The colors of the sun were in the lime-bright young beech leaves and the yellowy new forsythia. He saw a golden pheasant break out of the trees, make a sudden ascent into the depthless cobalt bowl of the sky.

He spoke English to the boy. "A blue sky for once! Do you suppose it's going to mean a bolt from the blue for me?" The towheaded youngster looked up at the sky as they walked along, but didn't reply.

Tixier-Vignancour was waiting on the other end of the line. Standing at the wall telephone in the hallway of Petersen's cottage, Céline watched a lazy fly circulate in a patch of sunlight a few feet above the polished floorboards. It revolved as slowly as a dust mote, catching the warmth of morning in its wings. This early in the year, even the flies still moved stiffly! When he heard Tixier-Vignancour say the word "amnesty," he felt his legs give out under him. He steadied himself against the wall. The sudden movement disturbed the logy fly, which lit off for a quieter haven.

On July 23, 1951,
Céline—with Lucette, and with five cats in a wicker basket
and the dog Bessy in a large plywood crate—returned to
Paris.

Friends who met the couple at the Invalides station were
shocked by the way Céline looked; in the seven years since
they'd last seen him he'd turned into an old man. He em-
braced them one by one. Then he asked if anything had been
written in the papers about his arrival. Someone hesitantly
handed him a copy of *l'Humanité,* folded open to a headline
bearing his name.

The story described the circumstances of his pardon, said

he'd been seen "strutting the Côte d'Azur," and concluded in summary judgment: "Notorious fascist, frenzied anti-Semite, Gestapo agent, creator of a gross literature of doubtful value, Céline was a great admirer of the Nazis, in whose service he has employed his nauseating pen ever since the Occupation of France."

After scanning the article, Céline crumpled the paper and threw it on the tracks. He laughed loud enough to turn the heads of travelers boarding a train on the next platform.

"I piss on them from a great height!"

ABOUT THE AUTHOR

Tom Clark was born in Chicago in 1941. He received a B.A.
from the University of Michigan and an M.A. from Cambridge
University, where he was a Fulbright scholar. He has received
grants for writing from the Rockefeller and Guggenheim
foundations and the National Endowment for the Arts. For ten
years in the sixties and seventies he served as poetry editor of
The Paris Review, of which he remains an advisory editor.
His books include many volumes of poetry from *Air* (1969)
and *Stones* (1970) to three volumes of selected poems, *When
Things Get Tough on Easy Street* (1978), *Paradise Resisted* (1984),
and *Disordered Ideas* (1987). He has written biographies of Damon
Runyon, Jack Kerouac and Ted Berrigan.
Tom Clark lives in Berkeley, California, with his wife and
daughter.